Two Sides of the Story

by
Mary Hooper

BLOOMSBURY

First published in Great Britain in 1998
Bloomsbury Publishing Plc, 38 Soho Square, London W1V 5DF

The moral right of the author has been asserted
A CIP catalogue record of this book is available from the
British Library

ISBN 0 7475 3578 7

Cover design by Mandy Sherliker

Printed in Great Britain by Clays Ltd, St Ives plc

10 9 8 7 6 5 4 3 2 1

CHAPTER ONE

Monday, 10th October

ASTRA

The first words I heard him say were: 'Is this Mrs Konya's class?'

Chelsea and I were sitting near the front of the room as usual, and we both looked up when the strange boy came in. I say strange, but I don't mean he was weird, just that he was a stranger. He was wearing our uniform – which isn't much of a uniform, just black jeans with a blue sweatshirt – and he was thin and dark and good-looking, with long, straight slicked-back hair and eyes which were slightly slanted.

He was speaking to me, but I blinked at him and didn't reply. I've never really liked – really *fancied* – a boy before and I was just struck dumb.

Under cover of the desk, Chelsea nudged me and made a squealy noise in her throat. The noise meant that she thought he was a hunk. I knew this because I'd heard it before.

'Yes, this is her tutor group,' she said to the boy eagerly. 'She'll be in in a minute.'

He nodded and stared from one to the other of us, slowly, gravely.

Chelsea said, 'Are you coming in here, then? You joining this class?'

'Yeah,' he said, and I felt my stomach give this strange little leap of excitement.

He looked round the class as if looking for somewhere to sit. Most of the boys are lumped near the back – they think they're not going to get noticed so much there – and they weren't taking much notice of the new boy. The girls, though ... well, more than a few of them were watching him. There was just something about him, you see. Something different. He wasn't like the other boys. He looked (and I could never tell Chelsea this because she'd have hysterics) like one of those old-time poets: thin and a bit tortured.

'I'll sit here, I reckon,' he said, and he moved towards an empty chair just in front of us. He sat down, stretched out his legs and began to whistle softly under his breath. He was so cool.

Chelsea nudged me again and made gleeful faces in his direction to indicate that she fancied him. This was nothing new, either,

Chelsea's always finding boys that she fancies: boys in the street; boys when we go skating; boys in the Aussie Soaps. They – the Soap stars she's mad on – are too brash and blond and loud for me, they fancy themselves too much.

If it comes to that, I don't reckon that boys in real life are much better: they're usually noisy and rude; always going on about sex and looking you up and down; then sniggering together. Chelsea and I don't like that.

Chelsea and I agree on all those sorts of things, and we make each other laugh, too, but we're different in other ways. She calls me a hippy because I'm interested in New Age stuff: star signs and crystals and omens; whereas she's a bit of a trendo: she's mad on clothes and whatever band's in at the moment – and she's completely potty on the Soaps, never misses a single one. I mean, I like them too, but she lives and breathes them. Once we had to spend a whole Saturday at the railway station because this Soap star guy was coming to open a supermarket.

A moment or two later Mrs Konya – Konnie – came into class and, because she was in a rush, sat down with the register and started calling it out without looking round the room.

I looked sideways at the new boy, wondering what colour his eyes were and dying to know what his name was, trying to think what he suited. Konnie didn't call out any new names, though. She got right to the end of the register and was just about to dismiss us when Chelsea said, 'Mrs Konya! There's someone else here!'

Konnie sighed under her breath. We were only three weeks into a new term and already our tutor room had been changed twice and four boys had been brought in from another group.

She looked across, saw the boy and frowned. 'Who are you?' she asked.

I held my breath. I wanted him to have a good name; I didn't want him to be called something fancy or posh or stupid.

'My name's Ben Adams,' he said, and I relaxed, pleased. Ben Adams, as a name, was near-perfect: straight, clean, uncomplicated. I printed Ben Adams on a new page in my rough book and wrote my own name underneath. I'd do a number check later to see if they matched.

I waited for Konnie to ask him his address and date of birth for the register. I wanted him to be an air sign, same as me – that would mean we went well together. Maybe, though, he'd be a fire sign. That would be OK too; it would mean we complemented each other: fire and air need each other to survive.

She didn't ask him anything like that, though, she just looked impatient. 'And where have you come from?' she snapped.

'Just moved to the area,' he said. 'I came to the nearest school.'

'Are you enrolled here?'

He gave a shrug.

Konnie sighed again, more loudly. 'Have your parents enrolled you?' she said impatiently, and I wanted to tell her not to speak to him like that.

'Shouldn't think so,' he said.

She hesitated for a moment, then the bell went for our first class and she slapped the register shut. 'You'd better go and see Miss Waters, the school secretary,' she said. 'Give her your details and get things organised.'

'I'll take you,' Chelsea said to Ben eagerly, before I could speak. I thought to myself then that it was funny she didn't say, *we'll* take you, when we always did everything at school together.

'You can go at break,' Konnie said. 'Just get off to your first lesson now.' She rummaged on her desk. 'I'll find you a timetable.'

We all bundled out of the room and as Chelsea went by the new boy – Ben – she made pouting, kissing movements behind his back. I smiled, but I thought to myself that he, Ben Adams, was worth more than this and that she shouldn't be messing around with him like she did with all the others.

We had Science next, a double period, but Ben didn't turn up for it so I don't know where he went. Although there are about twenty-five of us in Konnie's tutor group, we don't always have lessons together, and in a big school like ours Ben could have gone into another room or wandered off outside.

At breaktime, though, he was in the yard. He was talking to Rich and Josh, two boys in class who've got a bit more going for them than some. When he saw us he waved, then broke away from them and came over.

My tummy scrunched up when Ben waved at me, and when he grinned at me it scrunched again. I put my hand in my pocket and held on to my crystal. It was supposed to bring me inner peace and luck in love, but until then I hadn't had much call for it – or not the *love* bit, at any rate.

'I was looking for you two,' he said to us. 'I've got to go to the secretary's office, haven't I? I've got to be enrolled and registered and date-stamped.'

You *two*, I thought. In class Chelsea had said

she'd take him to the secretary, but he'd said he'd been looking for *both* of us. So that meant he must like me. Did he like me better than Chelsea, though? Suddenly it became massively important that he did.

Chelsea gave him one of her smiles. One of the mocking, flirty smiles she always gives to boys she fancies.

'Just follow me,' she said, and she was speaking all funny too: deeper and huskier.

We went into the school building and towards the secretary's office. The corridor was just wide enough to take the three of us together, with Ben in the middle.

'Ole Waters is a right misery guts,' Chelsea said.

'We call her Stormy,' I put in, and when Ben looked at me quizzically, added, 'Stormy Waters.'

He grinned, and was still smiling down at me when Chelsea put her hand on his arm and said something funny – and rude – to distract him and make him look at *her*.

When we got to Stormy's office, Chelsea and I said we'd wait for him so we could all go to the next lesson together, then Ben knocked and went in while we hung about in the corridor. Once he was inside, I pressed my ear to the door to try and hear what was being said, still hoping to hear what his birth sign was.

Chelsea took the mick out of me a bit then, about how I was acting with Ben, and when I said that I fancied him, she said that she fancied him as well. At the time, this didn't worry me: she gets crushes on boys all the time, and that she should fancy Ben was only natural, seeing as he was *the* most fantastic-looking guy. What was important to me was knowing that she didn't fancy him the way that I fancied him. *I* fancied him for real.

After about five minutes of waiting, I began to get a bit twitchy about getting to class, because I had some writing-up to do from last week's lesson.

I looked at my watch. 'I'll be in trouble with Besty if I don't finish my assignment,' I said to Chelsea.

She shrugged. 'Go if you want,' she said. She bent right over so that her head was upside down and her hair was touching the floor: she does this to give it body, make it fluff out. When she straightened up it was all round her head in a big wispy cloud. 'Ben will probably be ages.'

I shuffled about for another few minutes. I didn't want to leave Chelsea there waiting for him on her own – but on the other hand I was already in trouble with Miss Best. In the end I had to go, although when I got to class I couldn't concentrate on what I was supposed to be doing.

Chelsea seemed to be ages and ages coming in. When she did she was on her own – no Ben – and she just breezed in, humming under her breath.

I called her over but she said she had to concentrate on something and needed to be on her own, and she stayed over the other side of class for the whole lesson.

It was funny, I thought, because in all the time we'd been best friends, it was the first time we'd worked away from each other. Something had already changed between us.

CHAPTER TWO

Monday, 10th October

CHELSEA

I saw him first. He came into Konnie's class and his eyes looked all round the room and then they rested on me. I thought to myself *wow*!

We stared directly at each other, just for a moment, and I knew immediately that he liked me. I know that sounds big-headed but it's not, I'm just being truthful. I haven't got masses of experience with boys, but I just *knew*. I also knew that I liked him, too. Fancied him like mad, actually, because he reminded me of a guy who'd just come into one of the Aussie Soaps. Only Ben was dark instead of blond, of course.

He came right in and asked me (*me*, out of everyone in there!) if this was Mrs Konya's class. I knew then that he was new to the school because everyone, everywhere, always calls her Konnie. I said it was, and then he came and sat right in front of me.

Well, in front of us – me and Astra – if I'm strictly truthful – but just slightly more over *my* side.

I nudged Astra and made a face in his direction, and then I wrote inside my rough book: *Gorgeous* or *what?!*, in a big heart with an arrow through it.

Astra gave a little *tut* under her breath, as much to say I was at it again, but she's a bit like that, a bit of a non-starter where boys are concerned. That's why you could have knocked me over with a feather when it turned out that she was after him, too.

I suppose that isn't so surprising if you look at Ben. For a start he's really good-looking in a thin and hungry kind of way, like someone who's had one too many late nights, and he's got longish hair, dark and shiny, whereas most of the boys in our class have got practically zero. He's not that tall, but he looks as if he could stand up for himself in an argument. Best of all, he looks an individual, different from the other boys, and as if he doesn't care two jots what anyone thinks of him. I got the impression that no matter whether I fancied him, or if Astra fancied him, or if every girl in our class fancied him, it wouldn't make any difference, it wouldn't make him big-headed. And if everyone hated him, then he could deal with that as well.

Anyhow, it was arranged that I would take him to Stormy, the school secretary's office, at break. After Konnie had finished with us we filed out and I looked round for him, just to chat him up a bit, but he'd disappeared. This is quite easy to do in our school as there are 1,500 kids and the teachers are always changing their tutor programmes or getting in supply teachers, so it's difficult for anyone to keep track. At break, Ben was in the yard, though, talking to some of the boys. When he saw me he left them and came over.

God, Astra was such a *wimp*. She just looked at him all soppy, kind of hanging on his every word and all that, and it was then that I realised that she fancied him too. Well, fancied him isn't the word – I was surprised she didn't drop a lace hanky on the floor and wait for him to pick it up. Straight out of *Sweet Valley High* she was, fawning and giggling and being fluffy.

Anyway, we took Ben to Stormy's office, warning him first that she was a bit of a nightmare. When the door closed behind him, Astra stuck her ear on it and tried to hear what was going on.

'Where d'you think he lives?' she said. 'I wonder when his birthday is? I bet he's an air sign, what d'you think?'

'You're the expert,' I said.

She looked at me all starry-eyed. 'He's really nice, isn't he?'

'Yeah, he's a bit tasty,' I said. 'I quite fancy him myself.'

'I think he's gorgeous.'

'No!' I said in mock surprise. 'You don't!'

She went a bit red. 'Is it that obvious, then?'

'Well,' I said, 'it would be more obvious if you had a tattoo across your forehead saying *Astra loves Ben*, but only just.'

She bit her lip. 'I didn't realise …'

'It's just that nowadays girls don't usually go into a dead faint if a boy speaks to them.'

'No, I know,' she said. 'And I don't normally, do I? It's just he's so nice and …' she looked at me hopefully. 'Do you think he likes me?'

'I don't know!' I said. 'D'you think he likes *me*?'

'I expect so,' she said. 'Boys always like you.' And then she went quiet and looked at the floor.

We waited a bit longer and she started looking at her watch. 'I've got to get to Maths early,' she said, 'I've got something to write up.'

'That's OK,' I said. 'I'll wait. I'll look after him.'

She hung around a bit longer, obviously torn between getting into trouble with Besty and leaving Ben in my clutches. Besty won, because in the end she said she *had* to go and she'd see me in a minute.

I was prepared to wait for him until half-way through next week if I had to, but it was only a couple of minutes after that that he came out.

'OK?' I asked. 'Did you survive?'

'Got on all right with her, didn't I?'

I raised my eyebrows. 'I don't know what's happened, then. She must be weakening.'

'Perhaps someone's poured some oil on her,' he said, and when I looked a bit blank, added, 'Geddit? Oil on troubled Waters?'

I laughed.

He looked up and down the corridor. 'So where's your other half gone?'

'Astra? She had to do some writing up before class.'

'Yeah?'

'She's like that,' I added. 'Bit of a nerd at school. Gets panic attacks if she doesn't get her homework in on time.'

We started walking along the corridor, me searching my mind for something to say. I wanted to find out more about him, but I didn't want to be too obvious about it. 'While you were in with Stormy,' I said after a moment, 'Astra was trying to listen to what was going on – she's just dying to know what star sign you are.'

'Is that important, then?'

'It is to her. Mad on stuff like that, she is.'

'Aren't all girls?' he said.

'Some …' I said cautiously. If he was even remotely interested in that sort of thing, then so was I. And if he wasn't – well, I didn't know my Libra from my Leo, did I?

'What sign is *she,* then?' he said half-jokingly. 'Not that I actually believe all that stuff.'

'Gemini,' I told him.

He shook his head. 'It's ridiculous, isn't it? As if anyone could predict what one twelfth of the population would be doing on a certain day.'

'Crazy!' I agreed. 'Just a load of tosh.'

He suddenly stopped dead. 'Where are we going?'

'Maths. Isn't that what you've got on your timetable?'

'Maybe,' he said. 'But I don't much fancy it.'

'So what *do* you fancy?' I said, and I gave him a long, cool look.

He smiled at me and I realised that his eyes were a fantastic greeny hazel. He was just going to reply when Stormy suddenly came round the corner. *And not from the direction of her office!*

My jaw dropped: he *couldn't* have been in to see her. He must have gone in there and just been sitting quietly on his own. No wonder Astra hadn't heard anything through the door ...

Stormy gave me a brief nod and went by.

Ben looked at me quizzically, head on one side so that his hair flopped over his eye. 'What's up with you?'

I opened my mouth and then closed it again. If I said anything I'd practically be calling him a liar; putting him on the spot could cause all sorts of awkwardness between us.

'Nothing,' I said.

He shrugged. 'Well, I don't fancy Maths, so I'm just going to go outside and kick a ball about.'

'OK,' I said. 'See you later, perhaps. See you in the canteen at lunch-time?'

'Sure.'

He went somewhere – on to the playing field maybe? – and I went on to Maths and Astra.

But we didn't see him in the canteen – or for the rest of that day, actually. And I didn't say anything to Astra about him not really going in to see Stormy. It made him all the more exciting; meant he had some sort of mystery about him. A mystery that I knew something about, and Astra didn't.

CHAPTER THREE

Friday, 14th October

ASTRA

Chelsea came round tonight. We usually see each other two or three evenings a week, and always at weekends, but this week it's been just the once.

She's been really funny with me at school all week, as if I'm getting on her nerves or something. I know what it is, of course: Ben. Usually, when she fancies boys, it doesn't affect me – I just stand by, listen to her rave on about them and wait for it to wear off, or for the next crush to occur. This time, though, it's different. This time I'm involved.

Ben's been hanging around with us a lot. He seems to prefer being with girls rather than boys; he's not into shoving each other about and telling dirty jokes like they are, so he usually just chats to me and Chelsea. It's hardly ever about anything personal, though. Chelsea said to me that it's like getting blood out of a stone, getting him to talk about his life.

It's obvious, though, that it's *us* he likes, more than the other girls. Which one of us, though, I don't know.

I feel funny about it really. Chelsea's still my best friend and always will be, but now Ben's around things have changed, and are changing still. He's made things difficult between us, even though we don't talk about him much – *can't* talk about him – he's there in everything we do. Sometimes I just feel I want to be on my own with him, so we can really get to know each other.

There are all sorts of things I want to ask him: about his family and his home and his starsign, and whether he's had a serious girlfriend before and that sort of stuff. And I just don't want Chelsea around when I ask. I want to know him better but I don't want *her* to know him better.

Tonight Chelsea was in a really bad mood. She came over at about six, and before she'd arrived I'd cut out a little pile of horoscope features. This is something we always do: collect the astrology columns out of the weekend papers and magazines, copy down the main things that are supposed to happen to us and then check the following week to see if they've come true.

Sometimes they have and sometimes they haven't, and sometimes they're so vague that they might have done. Anyhow, we always do it. This week I'd read mine as soon as I'd cut them out because I'd been dying to see if they said anything about meeting someone special. About meeting Ben, in other words.

Mum let Chelsea in and I heard them chatting downstairs in the hall. Mum likes her, but I think she disapproves of her a bit – or at least she disapproves of her being allowed to do practically anything she wants and being given everything she asks for. Mum says it's easy for Chelsea's mum and dad: they've both got high-powered jobs and bags of money, so they can afford to 'indulge' Chelsea, as Mum puts it.

When Chelsea came into my room I had the cuttings ready on my desk. There was a little pile of *Gemini* – me, and a little pile of *Leo,* which is her.

'You'll never guess!' I said, because of course I'd looked at mine already. 'Quite a few of mine say something about Ben."

'What d'you mean?' she said crossly, and she pulled off her leather jacket and just flung it down on my bed, causing a gust of air and sending the cuttings fluttering to the floor.

I didn't say anything, just bent down to

pick them up.

'Well,' I said, reading one out, 'this one says, *Someone comes into your life who will become increasingly important as time goes by*, and this one in says, *A major change in your life is forecast by the arrival of someone new* and this one …'

'What a load of rubbish!' Chelsea said. 'You're not saying you really believe that stuff, do you? How many times have we checked up and nothing's come true?'

I shrugged. 'Sometimes it does.'

'Believe them and you'll believe anything,' she sniffed. 'You'll be telling me next that John Lennon works at the chip shop.'

There was a funny silence between us.

'Well, let's see what yours says,' I said after a moment. 'Maybe you're going to have an important change in your life, too.'

Actually, I'd already looked, and hers were really boring – all about people in authority getting at her and having to make provision for the future and stuff like that. Nothing about new relationships at all.

She glanced at one or two and then she looked at me with a sort of withering look on her face. 'They're stupid. I don't know why we ever bother to look at them. It's so immature, believing in fortune-telling and stuff. And as for all that weirdo crystal business – well, honestly, how can having a bit of glass in their pocket make any difference in anyone's life?'

'You've never said so before,' I said, thinking to myself that she wouldn't have said that if the horoscopes had said that someone new was coming into *her* life.

I pushed the cuttings to one side to look at later. 'Well, what d'you want to do, then?'

'Dunno,' she said moodily. 'What're you wearing to the party?'

The party was for our friend Sarah's birthday and was in a couple of weeks' time, during half term. Before Ben had arrived at school, we'd talked about it a lot. I'm not mad keen on parties – not like Chelsea – but I knew that it was expected that I should (a) be desperate to go, (b) have a fantastic time when I got there and (c) rave about it afterwards.

'I thought about going to the charity shop,' I said. 'Last time I looked I saw quite a few things I liked: long, black, slinky things.'

She raised her eyebrows. 'You and your old hippy clothes,' she said. 'You're getting to be a right weirdo. You'll have rings on your toes and feathers plaited in your hair next.'

'Maybe I will,' I said, trying not to to get riled. 'Trendy stuff doesn't really suit me.' I looked at her a bit enviously when I said this:

Chelsea's got quite a nice figure whereas I'm straight as a bean pole. She's got that lion's mane of hair, too, and a pink and white complexion, whereas I look sallow and my hair's as straight as a ruler. 'What're *you* going to wear to it, then?"

'Haven't decided,' she said, and then we said together, 'D'you think Ben will go?'

We both laughed falsely.

'I *hope* so,' Chelsea said, and then she added, 'I've already asked Sarah to ask him.' She said this as if it meant that because she'd arranged the invitation, he was going to be hers for the evening.

And then we were both silent again and I knew what Chelsea was thinking, because I was thinking it, too. It was: at the party let him talk to me and dance with me and even – maybe – kiss me. Not *her*.

She left early. We'd just done one of the number games – where you change the letters in people's names into numbers and then add them up to work out what their basic number is. It had worked out that my number was exactly the same as Ben's.

When I announced this, she pushed the paper away and gave me a disgusted look.

'Oh, it would be, wouldn't it?'

'What d'you mean? I haven't made it go like

that. That's the way it is – Ben and I are both number six.'

'Oh, so what?' she said. 'Ben and *I* have got the same colour eyes. What does that mean?'

'I don't know,' I shrugged.

'No, of course you don't.' She stood up and stretched. 'I'm off home,' she said.

'Already?'

'I've got things to do,' she said, and she went out, charged down the stairs and slammed the door behind her, leaving me just standing on the staircase.

Mum popped her head out of the kitchen. 'What's wrong with her, then?' she said. 'Had a row, have you?'

'Of course not,' I said.

She laughed. 'I was joking. You two have never had a row, have you?'

I shook my head.

'That's the way,' she said. 'There's nothing like best friends. If you find a good one, you'll be best friends for ever. They last much longer than men, believe me!'

I nodded. Maybe, I thought. And then I went back upstairs to read my horoscopes again.

CHAPTER FOUR

Friday, 14th October

CHELSEA

It's been a weirdo sort of week. Astra's really been getting on my nerves, whinging on about Ben all the time and worrying when he doesn't appear, and making great soppy eyes at him when he does. She keeps doing all these childish *he loves me, he loves me not* things, too: number games and throwing apple peel over her shoulder and pretending it's gone into a 'B' – rubbish like that.

I've told her that boys don't like girls who are a pushover and who make it obvious that they fancy a boy, and that she's going to turn him right off if she carries on that way, but she doesn't take a blind bit of notice. 'I'm just being myself,' she says. 'Why should I pretend to be any different? Besides, he's not like other boys.'

She's right about that. He's not like any of the other boys I've ever known. He's different, more private, more self-contained. The other boys are mostly so cocky and confident, so swaggeringly sure of themselves that you know that actually they're not at all sure, but Ben's so cool and laid back that you know he really is. If that makes sense.

I'm not going to bother any more to tell Astra how to act, I'm just going to let her get on with it, let her be soppy over him and turn him off. Telling her how to act with boys is just force of habit, I suppose, because I've always been the one with the boys round me. I flirt with them and play up to them and they love it, whereas Astra's what I think they call a late developer. She just hasn't been interested until now.

I've been trying to get Ben on his own all this week to chat him up a bit, but what with Astra glued to me like sticky-back plastic it's been impossible. Besides, Ben seems to come and go as he likes, just turns up for lessons when he feels like it, so it's never easy to work out where he's going to be at any given time. I've been trying to work out why he didn't go in to see Stormy, just pretended to, but I haven't come up with anything.

The best way of getting to know Ben, of course, would be to meet up with him out of school, but I haven't even been able to find out where he lives. I drop hints, but he doesn't follow them up. When I do find out, I'm going to have a little trip there, walk up and down outside and just *happen* to be there when he appears. Easy.

What will really get things moving will be Sarah's party at the end of the month – I don't reckon there's anything quite like a party for flinging yourself about a bit and getting your hands on boys. That's a couple of weeks' away though, and I want something to happen *now*.

I spoke to Sarah yesterday about inviting Ben to it.

'I'm not sure,' she said. 'I've already gone way over on numbers. Mind you ...'

'Exactly,' I said. 'It's not every day we get a new boy in class who's drop dead gorgeous.'

'Not that it's going to do me much good,' she said. 'It's you two he's interested in.'

I made a face. 'Us *two*?'

'Sometimes I think it's you he fancies, sometimes I reckon it's Astra.' She grinned, 'In a way, you and Ben are quite similar, you know ...'

'How d'you mean?' I asked eagerly.

'Your personalities – you're both leaders, both quite confident. I just feel you're in tune.'

'Does that mean we're made for each other?' I joked.

'Maybe!'

'Well, then,' I said. 'Invite him to your party and then we'll all find out.'

'I don't know,' Sarah said. 'My dad's really worried about gate crashers, and we hardly know anything about Ben, do we? He might tell half the town.'

'He doesn't know anyone round here,' I said. 'He comes from …' I hesitated, 'I don't know where he comes from, but it's not round here, so that's OK. If he doesn't know anyone, he can't tell anyone, can he?'

'Mmm …' Sarah said thoughtfully.

'He's a real laugh!' I pleaded. 'And honestly, he doesn't know a soul!' As I said this I wondered if it was true. It could be; we just didn't know. 'We're the only friends he's got!' I finished.

Sarah laughed. 'OK, you've convinced me,' she said. 'I'll give him an invite next time I see him.'

I did think about not telling Astra that Ben was going to the party. I had a bit of an idea that if she didn't know he was going, then she might – just possibly and if I talked her out of it – not go herself. She's not really a party animal. And with her out of the way and me dressed to kill, well, who knew what might occur?

As it happened, though, I didn't keep it to

myself for long: tonight at her house I blurted out that I'd got him an invite. Well, she'd been so stupid over her horoscopes, turning *everything* she read into meaning that Ben fancied her (and, natch, didn't fancy me) that I got really cross with her and just came out with it. Well, honestly, even if the stupid horoscopes *did* say things like that, I don't believe they'll come true. They're just a load of rubbish; someone sits in an office and makes them all up, everyone knows that.

The other thing that annoyed me tonight, if I'm honest, was that Astra looked really pretty. I wasn't feeling ravishing – my hair had gone frizzy in the rain on my way round, and I felt quite big and lumpy – and I just looked at Astra sitting there, with her dark eyes and straight shiny hair, and had this sudden feeling of horror that Ben was going to fall madly in love with her.

That really *did* cheese me off and I almost hated her for a moment. I made an excuse and came home.

When I got home I wished I hadn't, because there was no one in. Mum and Dad both work late nearly every night and though sometimes on a Friday they make an effort to get in early, tonight they'd obviously found something better to do.

I played some CDs downstairs and then I went to my room and watched videos of all my best Soaps. I love them, specially the Aussie ones; I pretend to myself that I've got a part in one, and that I'm famous.

I'm dead keen on acting. There's a drama club just started at school to put on a play once a year, and I'm going to join that, and Mum says I might be able to go to acting school later, after I've done my exams. If I don't do acting then I might be a model. I've sent off for details of a modelling school and I'm just tall enough.

Later on, Dad came in, and then I had a bath and went to bed. I tried to forget about Ben, tried to forget about Astra. I thought about being *me*, Chelsea Matthews, superstar and model. Best friends? Who needs them? ...

CHAPTER FIVE

Tuesday, 18th October

ASTRA

School was over for the day and I was sitting on the wall outside with Ben.

It was just about the first time I'd managed to be on my own with him. He was sitting so close I could feel the warmth of his body through his sweatshirt, and I was feeling good. More than good – fantastic. As if something wonderful was going to happen at any minute.

I turned my face up to the sun and swung my legs happily. Right then I wouldn't have changed places with anyone in the world. OK, I knew that any minute Chelsea was going to come out and spoil things, but until she did …

I turned to Ben. There was something I really wanted to ask him. Well, several somethings, now that I had him on my own. 'Are you definitely going to Sarah's party?' I said. 'I know you've got an invite.'

He nodded. 'I reckon so.' He seemed to

hesitate. 'Although I'm not that good at parties.'

'Nor am I!' I said eagerly, wanting to show that we had something in common, and really pleased he was telling me something about himself when Chelsea wasn't around. 'I don't like having loads of people around all at once. You feel you have to amuse everyone, don't you? And I can never think of anything original to say.'

'Exactly,' he said, and he gave me a smiling, sympathetic look which said he understood absolutely and was right with me.

'Chelsea's great at parties,' I went on, 'she flits about like a blue-whatsit fly and goes home having chatted up everyone in the place.' As I said this I felt a bit horrible, I was making her sound like a right slapper. 'Some people are just good at parties though, aren't they?' I added.

Ben nodded. 'Some people are party people.' His slanty, green eyes looked straight into mine, 'But you and I are different, aren't we? You and I prefer people one-to-one. Sometimes it's only that way that you can really get to know another person.'

I swallowed nervously, suddenly feeling all breathless. 'Well, that's air signs all over,' I gulped. 'I expect you're an air sign.'

'I am,' he said. 'And don't tell me – you are too, aren't you? Bet you're a Gemini.'

My jaw dropped. I was *amazed*. 'How did you work that out?'

'Ways and means. Working out people's star signs is a bit of a secret trick of mine. I live with my gran, you see – and she's psychic. She's taught me all sorts of things.'

'Really?!' I gasped. 'How fantastic.'

Better and better, I thought. Not only was he the most wonderful boy I'd ever met, but we had loads in common. When*ever* did you meet a boy who was interested in astrology and who could work out a girl's birth sign?!

'Look, I trust you to keep quiet about this,' he said. 'Everyone will think I'm some sort of freak if they find out I can work out birth signs and live with my psychic gran.'

'Of *course* I won't say anything,' I said. I glanced towards school and saw Chelsea coming towards us across the playground. There was loads more I wanted to ask, but it would have to wait.

'Look, I made you something,' I said quickly, and I fumbled in my bag and pulled out the friendship bracelet I'd been working on all weekend. I'd been waiting for a moment like this, when Chelsea wasn't around, to give it to him.

He looked at it and seemed to hesitate so I added, 'It's OK, boys do wear them.'

'Yeah, 'course they do,' he said. He held out his hand and I dropped the bracelet into it.

He studied it. 'You've made it well,' he said. 'Beautiful colours. It's sweet.' He looked up at me, 'like you.'

I stared at him, stared into those green eyes and felt all swimmy inside. 'I … I …' I began, and I don't really know what I was going to say, or what might have happened next, if Chelsea hadn't suddenly arrived behind us and given me a great slap on the back.

'Ouch,' I said irritably, feeling so cross I could hardly look at her. It had been a special moment, *our* special moment, and she'd ruined it. If she hadn't come up, anything might have happened. He might have kissed me.

I looked at Chelsea coldly, feeling guilty again as I did so. Chelsea and I had never fallen out, never been cold with each other before.

'Ask me, then!' she said.

'Oh yes, sorry,' I said, remembering. 'How did you get on?' I turned to Ben, 'Chelsea stopped behind to see about being in the school play,' I explained.

'Well, I'm in!' she said. 'Mr Bryant said he

can't *promise* that I'll be the star of the next production, but he'll see what he can do.' She ran a hand through her hair so that it was all messy and tousled. 'He said there are some parts that would really suit me …'

'You act then, do you?' Ben asked her.

'Well, I want to! I've always thought I could.'

He nodded. 'Great,' he said. 'I guess you're the type, eh?'

I smiled secretly to myself. Did he mean what I thought he meant: she was the show-off, pushy type?

Ben and I slid off the wall and the three of us started walking along together, Ben in the middle as usual.

Chelsea looked at me sideways. 'So what were you two chatting about?' she asked.

'Oh, this and that.' I was trying to remember everything, every single thing, to take home and think about later.

Ben opened his hand and showed her the friendship bracelet. 'Look what Astra made me.'

Chelsea stretched out her own arm. 'Snap!' she said. 'Look what Astra made *me*.'

But it wasn't quite snap, because Chelsea's bracelet was just plain whereas Ben's was five colours and a complicated Aztec pattern, with tiny little beads woven into it.

'Looks like I've got the de-luxe version,' Ben said, and we all laughed. Or tried to. I guiltily thought that I'd never bothered to make Chelsea such a nice one. I hoped she hadn't noticed I'd gone red.

We carried on walking home. Chelsea and I both live about a mile from school; sometimes we get the bus back and sometimes we walk, according to how we feel. This was a real breakthrough, though, because we'd never managed to get Ben walking home with us before.

We crossed the main road, our paces exactly matching each other's, chatting all the way. Chelsea was doing most of it, of course; I've never realised before how much she likes to talk about herself. A couple of times she turned to Ben and said something that I couldn't hear, and once I had a horrible suspicion that they were holding hands, so I deliberately dropped something and hung back to pick it up. When I looked, though, they weren't – I'd just imagined it.

'So, Ben, where do you live exactly?' Chelsea asked, coming out with it at last. Although we'd dropped lots of hints about it, neither of us had asked him straight out.

He made a vague gesture off to the right. 'Around,' he said. 'Over there. I don't know the roads so I'm not exactly sure until I get there.'

'Big House? On the Oakwood estate?' Chelsea asked. She sounded dead casual but I knew she was as desperate as I was to know.

Ben shook his head. 'Not there.'

There was another silence.

'So where did you live before?' I asked, because all he'd said was, 'Up the motorway a bit' or 'North from here,' when we'd asked.

He stopped walking. He looked from Chelsea to me and back again, then he said, 'One thing you ought to know about me: I'm a very private person and I've got certain reasons for not letting anyone know my business.'

'Sure!' Chelsea said quickly.

'We didn't mean to pry,' I added. 'We were just interested.'

'I might tell you the whole story sometime,' he said, 'when we know each other a little better.' As he said this his fingers brushed against mine and I shivered with excitement. It was obvious he'd meant that remark for me, not for Chelsea. It was *me* he wanted to know better.

We carried on walking, talking about the party and other things, Chelsea and I both careful not to pry.

In spite of what he'd said, in spite of being *almost* sure that it was me he fancied, I began to feel worried. I had to turn off to the left, soon, go round the crescent and into the close where I lived. Chelsea, though, had to go further – in the direction Ben had indicated. This meant, of course, that she'd be on her own with him.

'Shall I come home with you?' I said to her as we neared my turn-off. 'Or d'you want to come round to my house?'

She shook her head. 'Mr Bryant said we've all got to read through the play we're going to do. I want to be ready for next week.'

'Only I thought we could work on our history project together,' I said casually. 'Just for an hour or so.'

'Keen, aren't you?' Chelsea said. 'I thought you hated that project?"

'I do,' I said lamely. 'I just thought …'

Chelsea looked at me. She knew exactly what I thought.

'No can do!' she said all jauntily, while I thought to myself how much I hated that expression. 'See you in the morning, OK?'

I nodded and stared at Ben miserably. How come the one time – the first time – in my life I'd found a boy I liked, my best friend liked him, too?

'See you!' Ben said as they went off, and Chelsea smiled and waved.

'Bye!' I called, as if I didn't have a care in the world.

When I got to the corner I looked back, and Ben waved his hand. With that wave he seemed to be saying that it was all right, it was *me* he liked, not her.

CHAPTER SIX

Tuesday, 18th October

CHELSEA

'Wake up, Chelsea!' Mr Bryant shouted across the hall. 'That was your cue.'

I jumped up. 'Sorry!' I said. My mind had been on other things.

I glanced down at the script and then, very slowly, I walked across the stage, trying to look as if I was broken-hearted. I flung my arms out imploringly. 'Don't go!' I begged Sarah, who was pretending to play my daughter. 'Don't leave me!'

There was a long silence, and then Sarah gave me an *if-looks-could-kill* stare. 'You are no longer my mother!' she said, and turned on her heel and walked off.

'OK!' Mr Bryant said. 'Good. You've each had a chance to read a few lines. Next week I want you here for a couple of hours so we can get through the entire play.'

'Will you be giving out the parts, then?' I asked. 'I'd really like to play the part of …'

'All in good time, Chelsea,' Mr Bryant said. He clapped his hands to get everyone's attention. 'You can get off home now – but I want you all to have read through the play by next week.'

There were murmurings of protest from some of the boys.

'Never mind about football,' Mr Bryant said. 'Anyone who wants a part in the play has to put that first. Before *anything* else.'

I was half-way to the door by then.

'That goes for you too, Chelsea. The play comes first. *"The play's the thing"* as Shakespeare so aptly said. So whatever's been on your mind while you've been with us today has got to take second place.'

'Right,' I mumbled. 'See you next week.' And then I ran for the door. OK, I wanted to be in the school play, but I wouldn't have arranged to go along to the hall to enrol if I'd known that Ben was going to be around. When Astra or I had suggested walking home together before, he'd always said he had something else on – either that or he just wasn't there at the end of the day. Today, though, I knew for a fact that he'd been sitting outside the school, with Astra, for fifteen whole minutes. She'd had all that time on her own with him. *Anything* could have happened.

I pushed open the double doors and looked across the playground. Sure enough, they were sitting together on the wall. Sitting much too close. I slung my bag over my shoulder; I'd put a stop to that straight away.

I broke into a run, charged up behind Astra and slapped her on the back.

She turned on me, really fuming, but from the look Ben flashed at me, I got the distinct impression that he was pleased I'd come along when I had; that I'd appeared just in time.

The three of us began to walk home together and I told them about the play: *The Face in the Mirror*, and said that I was expecting to get a good part. Ben said he was quite interested in the stage, and he also said that he thought I was the right type to make an actress. I took that to mean that he thought I had presence – star quality.

Even better: when I told him that I was thinking about doing a modelling course if the acting didn't work out, he squeezed my hand briefly and said that I had great legs. Astra didn't hear him say that, but I'm going to make sure she finds out soon.

And as for Astra – well, I don't think I've ever realised before that when it comes down to it, as far as boys are concerned, she really hasn't got much going for her. All right, she can talk about her soppy stars and do the Magic Meg bit, but she can't chat to boys properly, not how they like to be chatted to. Another thing: she's got a nice face and lovely hair and everything, but she's not what you'd call *exciting*.

She asked Ben about where he lived, and where he came from before that, but she didn't get much out of him. I didn't question him too much – especially after he said something about being a private person. Anyway, I'd decided that I was going to ask the things I wanted to know when Astra wasn't around. And as she had to turn off for home before I did, that was going to be pretty soon. She was going to have to leave me on my own with him …

She really didn't want to do it. She thought of all sorts of reasons why she should come to my house. And when those didn't work, a few more reasons why I should go round to *hers*. As if I'd fall for that!

In the end, though, she had to go off, and Ben and I went on our way. *On our own at last!*

'I hope you didn't mind us asking about where you lived and everything,' I said once she'd disappeared.

'Girls can't help being nosy,' he said.

I grinned. 'Interested, I call it. Not nosy.'

'It's not that I'm being unfriendly or anything. I mean, I do want us to be friends, don't get me wrong ...'

I nodded encouragingly.

'But I've got some reasons why ...'

I touched his arm. 'I won't tell a soul anything you say. Honestly. I won't even tell Astra if you don't want me to.' I *especially* won't tell Astra, I thought. I struck a pose. 'Your dreadful secret will be safe with me!'

'Well,' he said slowly, 'it's not so much *my* secret, as my dad's.'

'Oh?'

'He's an actor, you see.'

My jaw dropped. 'No! Is he famous? Would I know him? What's he been in?'

'Oh, in loads of TV plays,' Ben said casually. 'He was a surgeon in that medical series last year. And he played a murderer in the prison six-parter before that. Yeah, he's quite famous.'

'What's his name?'

'His stage name is Mike McGovern.'

I thought hard. 'I think I've heard of him!' I said excitedly. 'I'm sure I have. Was he in that police series?'

'Yeah, that's him. Good looking bloke. About forty.'

'How fantastic!' I could hardly believe my luck! Here was I, all set for an acting career, about to get off with someone whose dad was a famous actor!

'It's really difficult for me, because he's paranoid about people finding out where he lives. He doesn't even like my friends coming to the house.'

'God!' I breathed. 'It must be great to be famous!'

'The house we lived in before got really well known, you see,' he went on, 'and we had people hanging round the house all day. My mum couldn't put the milk bottles out without finding someone camped on the doorstep.'

'No!'

'We even found a newspaper man going through our rubbish.'

'Wow!' I said. 'Fancy that. And do you get to go to any premieres and events and stuff?'

'A few,' he said. 'It's no big deal to me now, though. I've grown up with all that.'

'I suppose you have,' I said, and I immediately pictured myself, dressed up to the nines in something plunging, hanging on Ben's arm at the première of a film in Cannes. *Oh wow …*

He suddenly stopped walking. 'Look, Chelsea, can I trust you not to say anything about this?'

'Of *course* you can,' I breathed. 'I won't say a word to anyone. But it must be *wonderful* to be in that sort of world. So glamorous.' A thought suddenly struck me. 'Hey, is that why you didn't really go and see Stormy?'

'What?' he asked, confused.

'Stormy Waters – the school secretary. Did you just pretend to see her because you didn't even want *her* to know who your father is?'

His face cleared. 'Yeah. That's right. These things spread like wildfire. She'd only have to make one call to the local paper and that'd be it.' He looked at me closely, 'But how did you know I didn't really see her?'

I giggled. 'Because she passed us in the corridor about a minute after you came out of her office!'

'Oh, right.'

I stopped at the end of my road. 'I go down here.'

Ben looked up and down the road. 'Nice houses.'

I nodded. I live in a fairly OK part of town, but I could see at once that Ben was used to that sort of area and that it was no big deal to him. God, he probably lived in a mansion!

'These houses are OK,' I said, 'but Mum really wants to move. She's desperate to have a pool in the garden.'

He nodded. 'Yeah, we've got a pool in our garden,' he said, 'and a gym.'

'Fantastic!' I said. 'God, you must lead such a glamorous life.'

'You get used to it. As a matter of fact there's drawbacks.'

'Like what?'

'Like because we're rich, my dad keeps me short of money.'

'What?!' I screwed up my face in amazement. 'Why?'

He shrugged. 'He's got some bee in his bonnet about his kids not coming by things too easily.'

'I see,' I said. 'I suppose he just doesn't want you to become a Hollywood brat.'

Ben laughed. He had the most gorgeous teeth, straight and even. I hesitated, then nodded towards my house. 'D'you want to come in and have a drink or something?' I asked.

What I was suggesting was strictly against my mum's rules. I was allowed to have Astra back, of course, if there was no one in the house, but boys were strictly forbidden. Who cared about that, though?

'Sorry,' he said, 'I'm going off to meet some mates from where I used to live.' He picked up my hand, swung it briefly in the air. 'Another

time, OK?' he said. And he smiled at me mean-
ingfully.

'Another time,' I said. And then I went home
absolutely on cloud nine. Astra? She didn't
stand a chance.

CHAPTER SEVEN

Sunday, 23rd October

ASTRA

I'm sure Chelsea knows something. I'm sure she and Ben had some sort of secret conversation when we left each other on Tuesday. I bet she even knows where he lives, knows and she's not telling me.

I usually see her on Saturdays; we nearly always go for a mooch around the shops. Since Tuesday, though, when she went off with Ben, things have been really odd between us and nothing got arranged. Usually we take it in turns to call for each other on school mornings, but one day she didn't call for me, and once I didn't call for her – and then neither of us said anything about shopping today. We've both been pretending to be busy-busy-busy at school when we see each other – and I just couldn't bring myself to ring her when I got home last night. Well, I thought, if she was *that* bothered she could have rung me.

Seeing as we didn't see each other yesterday, I wasn't sure if she'd turn up today, either – we've got this long-term arrangement that she always comes over on Sunday afternoons. Sunday is my mum's big bake-up day, when she does what she calls a cook-in: scones and banana loaves and her own bread – stuff like that. Chelsea can't get enough of it, her mum isn't exactly what you'd call *homely*.

I didn't know whether I wanted Chelsea to come round or not. One part of me wanted her to, because I wished for things to be right and normal between us, but another part knew that it couldn't be right and normal any more, only strained and horrible ...

I suppose she must have felt the same. Anyway, she turned up about three o'clock, and for a little while we were both made an effort to be normal and it was all perfectly all right, just like we were before Ben. Mum gave us a plate of stuff: apple sponge, treacle tart and a slice of shortbread, and we went to sit at the bottom of the garden and eat them.

Away from Mum, though, we both dropped the best friends' act, and Chelsea got dead funny. She kept smiling secret smiles and dropping things into the conversation I didn't really understand: 'I guess best friends should be prepared to take a back seat if someone special comes along' and 'I hope I'd be unselfish enough to stand down if ever I was in the way' – things like that.

After about half an hour it began to drizzle, so we went up to my bedroom and put some tapes on. We talked about things, but not the way we usually did. It was like talking to someone on the other side of a glass wall. Neither of us wanted to bring up the subject of Ben, but he was there all the time.

I was still *dying* to know what had happened on Tuesday, but it was ages before I could bring myself to say anything about it. I wanted it to sound all casual and as if I couldn't care one way or the other, but of course it didn't come out like that. I just suddenly just blurted out, 'So did you go straight home on Tuesday?'

She looked at me and didn't say anything. Her face was entirely blank and expressionless.

I swallowed. 'What I mean is, did you … er … chat about anything with Ben? Did you find out where he lives?'

She carried on looking at me steadily. Then she said, 'You heard what he said – about being a private person. I don't think he wants anyone else to know where he lives and I think we ought to respect his privacy, don't you?'

Such a high and mighty tone she took. And the way she said 'anyone else' convinced me that she knew more than she was saying. Knew, but wasn't telling me …

I was so angry I couldn't bring myself to look at her. I tried to remember my yoga breathing techniques so I wouldn't lose my temper. OK, I was holding back on something *she* didn't know – about Ben's granny – but that sort of thing wouldn't interest her anyway.

'Oh well, I suppose he'll tell us in his own good time.' I said.

I hesitated, still niggled because she'd got the better of me, and couldn't resist adding, 'Anyway, while we were waiting outside school for you, we found we had loads in common.' I was surprised at myself as I said this. It was the 'my dad's bigger than your dad' thing, as if we were five again.

'Mmm?' she said, and she smiled to herself as if to say that it couldn't be anything worth bothering about. I was torn between telling her something she didn't know and keeping a secret. In the end, typical Gemini, I went halfway.

'As a matter of fact, he's really interested in astrology and stuff like that. And his granny sounds *so* interesting.'

'You don't say,' Chelsea said. She picked up one of the magazines she'd brought with her and started flicking through it. 'Sarah said the other day that she thought Ben and I were really alike in character. I suppose we are, really – don't you think so?'

I shrugged. 'Never thought about it.'

'We get on so well, too. Same sense of humour – that's really important, isn't it? Made for each other, I reckon.'

I was stumped for a moment, then I said. 'OK, if you two are similar in personality, then you might as well say that Ben and I are opposite. And you know what they say – opposites attract!'

'Huh!' Chelsea said. Just like that, in a dismissive way, 'Huh!'

She suddenly held up the magazine. 'There's a quiz here!'

'What about?'

'*How to find out if he fancies you*' she read out.

Well, she didn't have to say who.

We started doing it, Chelsea reading out the questions and both of us scribbling our answers on pieces of paper. There were ten questions, things like, *Do you ever look up to find that he's looking at you?*; *Does he say you look nice when you know you look grotty?* and

Does he laugh at your jokes?

You had to say whether it was: *All the time, Sometimes, or Never.*

At the end, when we added up the scores, they were both identical: twenty-five points each.

'Identical scores. There's a surprise,' Chelsea said, for she knew, and I knew, that we'd both fiddled our answers in order to get the best possible scores.

'And the million dollar question: *does* he fancy us?' She picked up the magazine again and read out, '*Mostly 'A's: He's absolutely nuts about* you*! He definitely thinks you're the girl for him. If he hasn't asked you out yet, he soon will.*'

She looked at me hard. 'So maybe he's nuts about us both.'

'But he can't ask us *both* out, can he?' I picked up the magazine and read out the fifth question: '*Does he notice things about you which no one else does*' 'What's he noticed about you, then?' I asked, trying to keep my voice curious rather than resentful.

'Oh, several things,' Chelsea said. 'What's he noticed about *you*?'

I smiled to myself, remembering. 'He said I was nice. Sweet.'

'Ah, how touching!'

I stared at Chelsea. I'd always found her sarcasm funny – but then she'd never used it on me before. 'So what did he say about *you*?'

'He said he'd never met anyone so interesting. He said I had fantastic legs. He said I was fascinating,' she said.

'Oh.' I swallowed. Fascinating, with fantastic legs, beat *sweet* any time. That's if she was telling the truth, of course.

She picked up her magazines. 'Well, better be off,' she said, getting up to go.

Usually she stays until eight or nine, but I bit back saying, 'Are you going already?' because quite honestly I didn't really want her there any more. I wanted to be alone and to think about the things she'd said.

'I'll say goodbye to your mum on my way out.'

I nodded.

'All's fair in love and war!' she said from the doorway.

'And may the best girl win!' I added.

She paused, 'Well, as you just so wisely said, he can't ask us *both* out, can he?'

She went downstairs and I stayed where I was, thinking deeply. Going out with Ben. An actual date. Could I really allow myself to think about that?

Neither Chelsea nor I had really been out with anyone on our own – not on what you might call a *date*. Chelsea had been out in a couple of foursomes, and she'd also had a few snogs with boys at parties, but I hadn't been out on foursomes or had any proper snogs. Nor even a proper kiss, only a silly one when a boy in our class and I had been messing about at a party. Our teeth had bumped and my lips had made a squeaky noise so it had been a bit of a disaster, and I'd already decided that it didn't count as a first kiss. I didn't want my first kiss, the one that I'd remember for ever, to have been one that squeaked.

But now I knew who I wanted for my first kiss and my first date: Ben. I wasn't going to be happy unless it was him. And if I had to lose my best friend along the way, then that was the way it would have to be.

I got up. And now I was just going to sit quietly and think about Ben, visualise him in my mind. They do say that if you think about things for long enough, actually visualise them happening, then they *will* happen. Well, that's what I was going to do, I was going to will him to choose me.

I lit one of the jasmine incense sticks I keep for special occasions and picked up my crystal. Holding it tightly in my hand I squeezed my eyes shut and thought about Ben for all I was worth.

Choose me! I urged him with every tiny piece of my body. *Choose me – not Chelsea!*

CHAPTER EIGHT

Sunday, 23rd October

CHELSEA

God, Astra was a drag today. I only went over to her house because I usually do, and because her mum always expects me over there on a Sunday.

She and I did a quiz about how to find out whether a boy fancies you or not, and she completely fiddled the answers so that she got the top score. I got the top score too, but I was being utterly truthful. I really *do* think Ben fancies me. There's this link between us, a connection. Sometimes, when I lie in bed and think of him, I just know that he's thinking of me, too.

Astra started asking me about one of the quiz questions, wanting to know what Ben liked about me. When I told her, though, she got all humpy. What I say is, why ask if she didn't want to know?

When I'd had just about enough of her cross-examintions I went home, much earlier than I usually do. It was all a bit awkward when I went downstairs – her mum appeared, obviously knowing something was wrong between me and Astra. I mean, I don't mind her mum, but she does like to stick her nose in.

She gave me a little greaseproof-wrapped parcel containing two slices of carrot cake. 'Something to nibble later,' she said. Then she added, 'You're going home early, aren't you? Is everything all right?'

'Oh yes,' I lied. 'I'm going early because I'm … er … going out with my mum and dad.'

'That's nice.' She smiled, 'Somewhere special, is it?'

'Just to relatives,' I mumbled, hoping she wouldn't ask any more. She knew me well enough by now to know that we hardly had any relatives – or none that my mum and dad bothered with, anyway.

She opened the front door and then put a hand on my arm. 'Chelsea, I hope you don't mind me asking, but is everything OK between you and Astra?'

I nodded, tried to look surprised at the question. 'Yes, of course.'

'Only she's been a bit funny lately. Edgy. I wondered if maybe you'd had a row or something.'

'Nope. No row!' I smiled at her brightly. 'See you in the week, I expect!'

'Yes, see you soon, Chelsea,' she said. 'Mind how you go.'

She waved to me all the way down the road, until I turned the corner and escaped.

Honestly, I thought. Talk about being on trial. First Astra, then her mum. It was just as well she didn't have a dad or he would have been there as well, probably quizzing me about my exam prospects.

I walked home. There was no one in, of course, the only sign of them was a note saying: *Darling – we've gone for drinks to the Kennedy's. Do come round if you want to.*

Oh yes, I thought. But how was I supposed to get there? The Kennedys lived miles away, out on the other side of the town. Besides, I hated them. They had a horrible horse-riding daughter and two stuck-up sons who played rugby.

I hung around the house for a bit, had a bit of a try of some of Mum's expensive new make-up, and then decided I might as well go out for a walk.

I suppose at the back of my mind I was thinking of Ben all the time, so when I set off walking I just automatically headed in the direction where he'd said he lived. There were about eight big, posh houses up on the hill, and I reckoned he lived in one of those. I had this vision of them all: Ben, his famous father and his elegant mother, entertaining lots of other TV stars. There would be drinks by the pool, champagne of course, and everyone would be dressed in the latest designer clothes and be incredibly glamorous. The fact that it was October and too cold to be standing around by a pool didn't matter. As far as I was concerned the vision was standard showbiz stuff; the sort of world Ben moved in. The nice thing about him, though, I thought as I walked, was that he wasn't a bit snobby or spoilt. Loads of showbiz kids are brats – you read about them in the papers all the time – but Ben wasn't.

I had him in my mind so much: the way he walked, the way he held his head, the way he looked at me with those slanty green eyes, that when I turned a corner and actually saw him walking towards me I was hardly surprised. It somehow seemed as if it was meant to be. It was that destiny business that Astra was always on about, but it was working for *me* this time.

My face broke into a smile when I saw him, and I just felt smilier and smilier the closer he got.

'So where are you off to, then?' he asked when we reached each other.

I shrugged, trying to sound casual. 'I'm just walking,' I said. 'I've been round to Astra's and I didn't fancy going home just yet.'

'Know what you mean,' he said. 'Parents get on your nerves sometimes, don't they? My dad's got some director over today and all he wants to do is talk shop.'

'So where were *you* going?'

He shrugged in an imitation of my shrug. 'I'm just walking,' he said. And he smiled.

My heart gave a great leap and all at once I felt fantastic. Of *course* it was me he liked. It couldn't be any other way. I couldn't feel like this without him feeling like it too.

We started walking towards the park. We talked about acting and about films and Soaps, about different boys at school and boys I'd been out with, about music we liked and – oh, everything. When I thought about our conversation afterwards, though, I couldn't remember much that he'd said about himself, so I suppose I must have dominated the conversation a bit. He was just so interested in me, though, he kept asking questions and was fascinated by it all: my childhood, my friendship with Astra, my family – everything.

When we got to the park he said he'd buy me an ice cream, but he hadn't brought any money out with him so I bought him one, and we sat together on a seat by the pond and ate them. When we'd finished and thrown bits of wafer to the ducks, he put his arm around the back of the seat. By moving closer to him, I could feel his arm all along the back of my shoulders and I knew that when I thought about it later, I'd be able to feel the warmth of his arm again, and imagine it was right around me ...

He said he'd buy me an ice cream next time, and then we started talking about money and he said a bit more about his dad keeping him short.

'It's ridiculous when you consider what he gets for a TV series,' he said. 'It's his way of trying to control me, though.'

'What d'you mean?' I asked.

'Well, for ages he's wanted me to go to some boarding school, where he went when he was a boy,' he said. 'I've always refused to go, though, so now he's making me do without my allowance while I reconsider.'

'God!' I said. 'Can't your mum say anything to him?'

'She wants to keep out of it,' Ben said. 'I mean, she slips me the odd tenner when she can, and that keeps me going.'

'What about clothes and stuff? How d'you manage?'

'That's just it. I used to have a store account and I bought whatever I wanted, but a few months ago my dad cancelled my card. Tell you what – I can't even buy anything decent to wear to that party of Sarah's.'

'I'll lend you some money!' I said, straight away. 'You can pay me back any time.'

He shook his head. 'No, don't be crazy. I couldn't do that.'

'Honestly!' I said. 'We've always got money hanging about at home. And I've got birthday money I haven't even spent yet.' I paused, 'They give me money all the time,' I said, and added bitterly, 'They give me money instead of being around for me.'

'I'm getting some money from my uncle,' he said slowly, 'but that won't be for a couple of months.'

'You could pay me back then. Go on – please!'

'No. It wouldn't be right.'

'Oh, *please*.' I really wanted to do something for him. And I also wanted him to come to Sarah's wearing something that I'd paid for …

'Well …'

'Let's go home right now and I'll get some! Will twenty pounds do?'

He didn't say anything so I added, 'Or have more! You might as well. I've probably got over forty pounds in my desk.'

'No, really. I don't want that much. Maybe just enough to last me until my uncle's money comes. But I'll give you a receipt or something ...'

I jumped up and, taking his hand, pulled him up. 'Come on. Let's go!'

When we got to my house my dad's car was back in the drive, so they were obviously home. I got Ben to wait at the end of the road and let myself in.

Mum and Dad were in the sitting room with the TV blaring out.

'Hi. I'm home!' I called, and I went straight to my room and got out the little cash-box I keep in my desk. I took out forty pounds in ten pound notes, and put it in an envelope. I was just going to stick it down when, on an impulse, I picked up one of the notelets Astra had given me. She'd bought me a CD for my birthday, but as a little extra she'd also bought some plain white cards and decorated them with rainbows and clouds and stuff like that. They weren't really my sort of thing, but they were quite cute; I used them for odd notes I had to write to people.

I hesitated, wondering what to write to him. I didn't want to be too sloshy, but I did want him to know how I felt. In the end I just wrote: *For Ben: This is our secret! All my love, Chelsea.* And I put three kisses and a little heart.

I put the card in the envelope, too. I looked in the mirror, put on some more lipstick, and hung my head upside down so that my hair was really big and frazzled, then ran down the road to where Ben was waiting.

As I gave it to him he began to protest.

'No! Don't say a word,' I said, and I put my finger on his lips. 'You can give it back to me any time.'

He looked inside the envelope, saw the card and took it out.

'This is terrific artwork,' he said, examining it closely. 'Did you do it?'

I was just going to say no, but he looked so impressed that I found myself nodding. 'Just a little hobby of mine. I really like drawing.'

'You've got talent!'

'Oh, it's nothing,' I mumbled.

'Beautiful, clever, funny, artistic,' he counted off on his fingers. 'Is there no end to your talents?'

I laughed. 'Nope!'

He put the card back in the envelope without reading it, and then put the envelope in his back pocket. 'I'll read it when I get home,' he said. 'And thanks a million. You're a really special girl, you know that?'

Usually when someone says things like this they're being clever or sarcastic, and I can usually come back with a smart retort. This time, though, I knew a clever reply wouldn't have been right.

He bent his head and kissed the end of my nose. I closed my eyes and waited for him to kiss me on the lips, but he didn't.

I opened my eyes, disappointed.

'See you at school,' he said, and he smiled and turned away.

I swallowed hard. 'Yes. See you.'

I took a deep breath to steady myself. There was no doubt about it. It didn't matter what Astra's stupid stars said, or how many quizzes she came top of, or what sign anyone was.

He was *mine*.

CHAPTER NINE

Wednesday, 26th October

ASTRA

'Hi!' I called. It was dinner-time and I'd just spotted Ben leaning up against the school wall, all on his own.

I went over to him, combing up my hair with my fingers as I went, trying to put a bit of bounce in it so that it looked fluffier, more like Chelsea's, and didn't just hang on the sides of my face like curtains.

I was really pleased to see Ben that morning because he hadn't been around for the past two days. Although one part of me said that he was an important person in my life and he *couldn't* have just gone out of it, another part was terrified that he had. I knew Chelsea was worried about where he was, too, but neither of us said anything. I think we were both trying to pretend that we knew something the other one didn't.

The funny thing was, in our paper that morning my horoscope had said, *Watch out for the conjunction of the moon with Aries. This means you'll be able to press home your advantage; your dearest wish could come true!*

So ... Ben on his own. Just what I'd been hoping for – especially as I knew that Chelsea had a dentist's appointment and wasn't going to be at school until the first class in the afternoon.

I'd spent yesterday evening going through my copy of *Love Signs in Astrology* just to reassure myself that Ben and I *were* alike and compatible as far as the planets were concerned. My book said (amongst other things) that 'two Geminis together are a marvellous combination, each understanding the other's dreams, desires and ambitions.'

Seeing this, I'd immediately copied the lines on to a piece of parchment in gold lettering, and decorated it with hearts and rainbows. I'd pinned it up over my bed and was going to look at it every night before I went to sleep.

Ben and I, two Geminis together, a marvellous combination. It sounded pretty good to me ...

I beamed at Ben. 'So where have you been for the last couple of days?'

He shrugged. 'I just couldn't be bothered to come in. Monday it was mostly Maths and Tuesday was stupid Woodwork in the morning with that Personal Development rubbish in the afternoon. Not my thing at all.'

He went on. 'I mean, last Tuesday we had that woman talking about us being programmed by our backgrounds into behaving as we do.'

'Is that what she said?' I didn't like to say that I could hardly remember, that I'd spent the whole of the lesson staring at the back of his neck and the way his hair grew.

'Behaving as if we've been programmed!' he repeated. 'Stupid! I don't think that. I think anyone can be anything he wants to be, don't you?'

I nodded. He stumped me sometimes with his thoughts and his ideas, but I nodded anyway. 'I guess so,' I said.

'Yeah, anyone can be anything he wants to be,' he repeated.

I struggled to get on to easier ground. It wasn't often that I got him on his own and I wanted to make full use of it. 'Tell me more about you,' I said. 'Your gran sounds amazing. Was she born psychic or did she sort of develop the gift?'

'Er …' He seemed unsure. 'Born psychic, I suppose. Although she didn't realise she was, until she started doing the tarot.'

'Fantastic!' I breathed. 'I've got a set of tarot

cards – I'm trying to learn how to use them. You have to be really careful with them, you know. You even have to put them back in their box in a certain way.'

'Yeah, I know that,' he said.

'Oh, sorry!' I said. 'Of course you'd know. Have you tried reading them yourself?'

'Just a bit,' he said. 'My gran's already told me I've got latent psychic gifts. I won't really develop them until later, though, apparently. Until I meet the someone who'll become really important in my life.'

'Who will that be?' I asked. 'You mean, like a teacher or a guru?'

He hesitated and smiled down at me, and though there were people all around us I felt we were completely alone.

'Maybe,' he said, and he leaned nearer and kissed me on the forehead. 'Or maybe just when I meet *someone*.'

My throat went all dry so that I couldn't even swallow. He meant *me*.

He looked down at me. 'Look, Astra, we're good friends, right. More than friends. And this is our secret, isn't it?'

'Of course,' I said hoarsely. I felt tingly all over. Where he'd kissed me, it burned.

'And you won't say a word to anyone else about me being psychic, will you?'

'Of course not!' I said.

'I mean, you know what blokes are like – if the wrong person finds out they'll just have a field day. I'll be down as the loony with the mad gran.'

'I think she sounds fascinating,' I said. 'I'd give anything to have someone psychic in my family.'

'Well, maybe you'll get to meet her some day. I'll ask her to read your tarot.'

'That'd be great!'

'We live in a pretty strange situation, actually. You'll have to make allowances …'

'What d'you mean?'

'Well, my gran's a full-blooded gypsy. Lives in a caravan – one of those proper Romany ones, you know?'

'How fantastic!' I said. 'I'd love to live like that. She travels about, does she? And that's why you got to school late in the term and everything.' And why you're so secretive about where you live, I thought to myself.

The bell went and we started to walk across towards school. He opened the door and we went in and along the corridor to our lockers.

I felt blissful – so glad that Chelsea was at the dentist!

I put a few books in my locker and then stood by Ben's while he sorted some things out. He handed me a plastic bag and asked me to hold it whilst he dropped a few school books in.

He then stood a couple of text books on the top of the locker and turned to speak to a boy called Luke, who was standing on the other side of him. While he was speaking I happened to glance at the text books – and saw what looked like one of my notelets sticking out of the pages.

I looked closer – yes, it was definitely one of mine. I'd decorated six for Chelsea; they'd been part of her birthday present. She must have sent one to Ben!

I froze, *desperate* to see what she'd written, and before I could think twice about what I was doing I'd reached up to the top of the locker, picked up the text books and dropped them into the plastic bag I was holding. As I did so I murmured, 'I'll put these in here, shall I?'

Ben was still speaking to Luke and didn't reply. Very carefully, very casually, I then put my hand into the bag, located the book, pulled out the card and slipped it into my jacket pocket.

My heart started pounding so fast that I could actually hear the beats. I don't know whether this was because I'd never done anything so awful before, or because I was just so anxious to see what she'd written. Both, I suppose.

Part of me said, *How could you?* and part said, *Quickly, find out!* Why had she written to him? What secrets did they have between them that I didn't know about?

Ben turned away from Luke and shut his locker with a bang, making me jump. We began to walk towards the swing-doors when suddenly he just turned to me and said, right out of the blue, 'Will you be in town on Saturday morning? D'you want to meet me?'

I stared at him. What did he mean? A proper *date*?

'Well … um …' I stuttered, not knowing what to say. Normally I would have agreed like a shot, but a couple of days before I'd arranged to go into town with Chelsea – we were supposed to be buying something to wear to Sarah's party next week. We hadn't seen each other for a couple of Saturdays so in a way I'd been quite anxious to go with her, to try and be normal and best-friendly again.

I opened and shut my mouth. I didn't want to tell him that I was meeting Chelsea in case he said that she could come along too. But on the other hand I wasn't going to turn him down flat – especially for someone who hardly had two words to say to me these days. *And* someone who was writing secret notes to Ben.

'If you've already got something arranged ...'

'No, that'd be great!' I blustered. 'What time and everything? Shall I come round for you?' As I said this I was thinking that I'd love to see the caravan and his granny and she might read my tarot cards. She might look into the future and say to Ben, 'This is the girl who is going to be the most important person in your life ...'

Ben shook his head. 'I've got a few things to do first, so it'd be easier to see you in town. How about meeting in the square about eleven?'

'Right!' I said eagerly. 'Great!'

I know the books say you're supposed to play it cool and everything, but I couldn't be like that. Ben had kissed me and asked me out and I felt I could have burst with happiness. *Your dearest wish could come true today ...*

But at the same time that card of Chelsea's felt as if it was burning a hole in my pocket. I was *desperate* to read it.

We made our way to the art room: we had Art for a double period, then a group of us were going swimming. Chelsea hadn't yet appeared, so I dumped my stuff on the side and then tore down the corridor and into the loo.

My hands were shaking as I locked the door behind me and looked at the card. There were only a few words:

For Ben: This is our secret! All my love, Chelsea.

I stared down at the card. *This is our secret*, I repeated to myself. What was? '*This* is our secret' – as if something else had been enclosed. What, though? A book? A newspaper cutting? A photograph of herself? How could I find out? I stared at it for ages, biting my lip and wondering.

In the end, not knowing what else to do with it, I tore the card up into tiny pieces and flushed them down the loo. I didn't need to keep it, I'd always remember what it said.

When I went back into class someone told me that Ben had gone off with a group who were supposed to be doing architectural sketches of the outside of the school building. Chelsea was in there, though, sitting on a side bench, swinging her legs. And from the secret smile on her face I guessed she'd just been speaking to him.

I went over and spoke to her but she was really horrible to me. Quite nasty. So in the end I just found something else to do and didn't work with her.

I wasn't going to worry about her any more. And I wasn't even going to worry about what the card meant. It was me who had the date with him, not her.

Saturday. I couldn't wait …

CHAPTER TEN

Wednesday, 26th October

CHELSEA

Ben was away from school two days this week, and I must admit I was worried. I didn't think he'd just skipped with my money – of course not – I just wondered if maybe his dad had suddenly demanded that he go to this boarding school and hauled him off. Or maybe his dad had started filming in some fancy part of the world and wanted his family to go along with him.

I didn't tell Astra any of my thoughts. I wasn't going to break my word and tell her what Ben had told me about his family and about his dad being famous. Besides, Astra's being such a wimp lately. I've not known her really fancy a boy before and I can't say it suits her; she's turned into a right drip, going red at the sight of him and fawning over him. Makes me sick, it does really.

Having Ben around has really changed things between the two of us. I mean, just a month or so back we were as close as any-thing, sharing every tiny thing we ever thought about. If we had a big event coming up – like Sarah's party next week – we'd have talked of nothing else but that, what we were going to wear to it and who was going to be there. This time, though, we'd hardly men-tioned it, apart from arranging to go shopping on Saturday for something to wear. Even that was a rather half-hearted arrangement, made more because we always *used* to go shopping on a Saturday rather than because we want to now.

I didn't get to school until dinner-time today because I had to go to the dentist, so I spent most of the morning at home reading *The Face in the Mirror* ready for the first read-through after school.

Going to the dentist was a rat, but when I got to the art room for the afternoon's first lesson, still feeling a bit funny after having two injections, the first person I saw was Ben.

My heart skipped a beat – it really did. He glanced up and saw me, and came straight over.

'Didn't see you at dinner-time,' he said.

'Didn't see you yesterday. Or Monday!' I retorted.

He grinned at me. 'Couldn't be bothered,'

he said. 'Besides, my dad wanted me to go to some studios with him. He was discussing a part in a TV series and ...'

I gasped. 'Really?! Did you see anyone famous?'

'No one that interesting,' he said. 'That red-headed girl – you know, that Soap star – was wandering about in the canteen. Don't know if you'd call her famous.'

'Wow!' I said.

He lowered his voice, because Sarah and a couple of the others were nearby. 'It's no big deal,' he said. 'I mean, when you see them close up, they're just like anyone else.'

'I know they are really, but ...' OK, I *knew* they were just ordinary people, but as far as I was concerned they were also stars. Just like in Hollywood, only on a smaller scale. They opened supermarkets and appeared at night clubs, they went to film prèmieres, got sacks of fan mail and everyone loved them. They were *stars* ...

'Your dad must be really well in with every-one,' I said. 'I bet he knows everything there is to know about acting, doesn't he? Bet he'd be able to give me a few pointers.'

'I bet he would,' Ben said. 'And maybe you'll meet him one day.'

I was just going to follow this up by asking

when, when Mr O'Neill, the Art bod, came in and, after a bit of chat, picked Ben and a handful of others to go outside and sketch features of the school.

'Hard luck,' I said to Ben. 'It looks like rain.'

He picked up some cartridge paper and a board. 'That's OK,' he said. 'As a matter of fact I'm quite pleased to get out of here. Your mate Astra is getting just a bit …' And he pulled a funny face.

'Just a bit what?' I asked eagerly, for I could tell that whatever it was, he didn't like it.

'Oh, you know – a bit clingy,' he said. 'She was hanging around at dinner-time and I couldn't seem to shake her off.'

'Do you want me to have a word with her?' I asked eagerly. *Back off, he's mine …*

He shook his head. 'No, that's OK. I can handle it. See you later, maybe? Walk home after school?'

'Yeah, sure,' I said eagerly, and then I remembered. 'Oh, there's the play reading. I forgot. But I could easily skip it, I mean, I …'

He looked at me in surprise. 'But you wouldn't want to do that, would you? I thought you were dead keen on this acting lark. You'll never get to be famous unless you work at it!'

'Yeah, I know that, but …' But I'd chuck it

all in for a chance to walk home with him – especially when he'd just talked about Astra coming on too strong.

'See you around, then,' he said, and he touched my shoulder, smiled and went off.

No more than a minute after, while I was still staring after him and thinking that he was just incredible, special, the best thing to hit the school since sliced bread, Astra walked in, looking flustered.

She came over and asked me if I'd seen Ben – if we'd spoken to each other at all.

I nodded. 'Oh yes. We had quite a chat.'

If the situation had been different, if it had been another boy who'd told me that Astra was getting clingy, I'd have said something to her. Nothing nasty, just dropped a hint to tell her to wise up a bit. With our situation, though, I wasn't going to. I wanted her to be as clingy as possible, as silly and drippy as she liked. I wanted him to go right off her, to find her a drag.

'A chat,' she repeated. 'What about?'

'Oh, this and that,' I said. 'I can't remember. What did *you* chat to him about?'

'What d'you mean?'

'Well, you've had more time alone with him than I have. You were with him all dinner-time from what I've heard.'

'Who told you that?' she said, going red. Then she said. 'Why are you being so horrible to me?'

'I'm not!' I said. 'I've just had two really grim injections, three fillings and my mouth feels like hell, so excuse *me* if I'm not exactly a laugh a minute.' As I spoke, I realised that I hadn't even thought about the dentist from the second I'd seen Ben. Still, she wasn't to know that.

Still red, she bit her lip and looked away. Then, although the two of us were supposed to be working on a project about print-making, she found something else to do, something with Mr O'Neill.

And we didn't talk to each other for the rest of the day.

After Art we were due to have a free period back in our tutor room, but then Konnie came in she said that instead of it being free, two local social workers were coming in to talk to us.

'About what?' one of the boys asked.

'Oh, this and that,' she said. 'Things which concern young people today: homelessness and staying on the right side of the law, things like that.'

'Drugs, sex and rock and roll?' someone else asked.

'Probably,' Konnie said.

She went out and while we were sitting there waiting for the social workers, Ben picked up his books and sauntered towards the door.

'You going out?' I asked him.

'I'm going home.'

'Why?' I asked in surprise, while Astra just sat there gawping. 'The social workers will be a doddle. We won't have to do anything except sit there and listen.'

'Social workers and me don't mix,' he said, and he just raised a hand and disappeared.

At three-thirty I went off to the play reading, which turned out to be a bit of a dead loss. I'd read through *The Face in the Mirror* a couple of times, but I hadn't learned any parts off by heart, which Mr Bryant seemed to think we should have done. Several of the really keen girls, like Janine and Imrie, *had*, so they were the ones who got the main parts to read.

'I won't be assigning parts for a couple of weeks yet,' Mr Bryant said when I asked him who was going to play the lead. 'I not only want to see who can act well, but also who shows the most enthusiasm for the play itself.'

I put a suitably keen expression on my face when he said that, though the main reason I wanted the starring role was to impress Ben. It would be so easy then to casually say that I'd love to meet his dad and get some acting tips …

It was five-thirty by the time we'd read right through the play and Mr Bryant eventually let us out. It was too late for any of the school buses by then, of course, so I set off home thinking about Ben, wondering whether I'd see him on his own to talk to before next Monday – Sarah's party. Most of all, I wondered what would actually happen at the party.

I was only a few hundred yards from school when Ben appeared.

'What are *you* still doing here?' I asked, my heart thudding. *He'd hung about to see me …*

'Things to do,' he said mysteriously. 'What were the Social like? What did they talk about?'

'Nothing much,' I shrugged. 'Mostly about leaving home and about how dodgy it is in London and all that.'

'Oh, right,' he said, and it may have been my imagination but he seemed to look relieved. 'So how was drama, then?' he asked after a moment.

'Great!' I lied, and then before I could stop myself, added, 'Bryant said I'm a natural. He reckons I could go far.'

'Fantastic!' He slung his arm around my shoulders. 'I'm glad I bumped into you on your own,' he went on, 'I was just thinking that I might go into town Saturday to buy something to wear for Sarah's party. D'you want to come with me?'

Did I?! I felt like leaping in the air. 'Saturday …' I said thoughtfully. 'Yeah, I think that'll be all right. Shall I come round for you?'

He shook his head. 'No, I'll meet you in town – in the square. Eleven o'clock all right?'

'Fine,' I said. Fine? Talk about that word being the understatement of the year!

We walked on, his arm still draped around my shoulders. I would have given *anything* for Astra to come along and see us.

I left him at the end of my road (I think he might have kissed me but people kept walking by) went straight in and picked up the phone.

'About Saturday,' I said to Astra. 'I won't be able to make it. I've got to go out with my mum and dad.'

'Oh, that's all right,' she said, cool as anything. 'I've got something else on as well, actually.'

'So that's OK, then.'

'Sure.'

'See you at school tomorrow!' I said in as friendly a voice as possible, and put down the phone.

Oh, it was going to be difficult, but she'd just have to face up to it. Ben and I had a date. It was *me* he'd asked out, not her …

CHAPTER ELEVEN

Saturday, 29th October

ASTRA

I was up at seven o'clock this morning and in the bathroom at half-past. Mum shouted to me, asking what was going on and what was I doing up so early when it wasn't a school day, but I just had my shower, using all my best Body Shop shower gels and creams, and then crept back in my bedroom. I looked outside to see what the weather was doing and then I started delving into my wardrobe, dragging out clothes and trying to make up my mind what to wear.

What was suitable for a day in town with the boy you fancied? Were we going to go shopping, or for a walk, or maybe (was it a real date?) for something to eat and then to the cinema? At school, Ben had only seen me in jeans and sweat shirts, but now I had a chance to show off a bit.

I just couldn't decide, and I felt myself beginning to get a bit stressed, so I put on a pipe music tape that I'd bought from the crystal shop and tried to calm down. I heard the newspaper arrive, got it out of the door and looked to see what they predicted for *Gemini* today, for me and Ben.

It said: *Life's difficult issues often turn out to be the most rewarding, and if you refuse to be downcast by what seems to be a setback, things may turn out to be for the best. Put your natural talents to good use, and you can't possibly fail.*

I folded it up again. It could mean *anything.* Of course, I knew that daily horoscopes were pretty vague and I was saving to have a personal horoscope done, but I didn't like the sound of. *refuse to be downcast by what seems to be a setback* … What did it mean?

I gave up on the horoscope and went back to worrying about what I was going to wear. After putting on about twenty different outfits, decided on a really long purple skirt a tie-dyed blouse and a black waistcoat with silver embroidery on it. I also painted my toe nails silver so you could see them through my thong sandals (I wanted to wear these, even though it was quite cold), and put on five different silvery necklaces. Once dressed, I darkened round my eyes with loads of kohl and put on some plummy coloured lipstick.

I brushed my hair and tried to make it look

a bit messy and more interesting with gel, then studied the whole effect in my bedroom mirror.

I sighed, unsure. I *thought* I looked OK – I certainly looked different from how I looked every day – but I really couldn't say for definite whether it looked right or was too over the top. Before, I'd always had Chelsea to ask; for years we'd always told each other what looked good and what didn't, but even if she'd been here now I wouldn't have been able to trust what she said. It was quite likely, the way things were between us, that she'd say I looked fantastic when I looked daft.

I studied my reflection again, trying to look at myself through *his* eyes. I nodded slowly … yes, I was fairly sure that a boy who lived with an eccentric old granny in a caravan would prefer to go out with a girl who dressed in an interestingly different way, rather than one who went along with high street fashion and looked like everyone else. Rather than someone like Chelsea, in other words.

I thought about Chelsea, glancing at the photographs of us that were pinned all over my notice board. They went way back: there were photos of us on holiday last year, photos of us at Chelsea's tenth birthday party, posing by the huge cake her mother had ordered from Harrods, and photos of us holding hands on our first day at playgroup.

When we were small Chelsea and I had looked quite alike: our hair was quite short then, and we'd worn it in the same style. We were exactly the same height and size and we used to wear the same type of clothes, too. Sometimes, when we were playing, we pretended we were sisters. The older we got, though, the more unlike each other in looks we became. But we still shared everything and were still best friends.

Now we don't look anything alike; I've got secrets from her and I don't even know if we're still best friends.

But *she's* got a secret, too. The card she'd sent him – what had it meant? Maybe, I mused, it was all on her side: Chelsea, coming on too strong again. She sometimes did that – went after boys and wouldn't take no for an answer. Last year she'd sent five different Valentine cards – and once she'd sat outside a boy's house all day waiting to talk to him, refusing to budge. In the end his mum had appeared and asked her to go home.

Maybe she was being like that with Ben; making a nuisance of herself. And Ben, being the sort of boy he was, didn't like to say anything to her in case it hurt her feelings. Maybe he'd say something to me. Perhaps I'd have to tell her, very gently, that he just didn't fancy her …

Once I'd finished doing myself up, I had to get out of the house without Mum seeing me, so I waited until she was in the shower, then shouted to her that I was going shopping and wasn't sure what time I'd be back. I didn't want to get into a discussion about what I was wearing, and *definitely* didn't want to get into a discussion about boys and dates and all that stuff.

I got to the square early – miles too early. I went into one of the big shops, agonised at myself in the loo mirror, wasted a bit of time spraying myself with perfume and looking at tights and then went out again.

It was eleven o'clock. As I walked back towards the square, holding on to the crystal in my pocket to give me the right vibes, I wondered to myself what it would be like when we saw each other. Would we be different out of school, and was this the beginning of a new sort of relationship for us? Should I kiss him on the cheek when we met, or would we hug, or would we not do anything – just be embarrassed and awkward with each other? Would it not be like any of those; would it be like in the movies where everything goes fuzzy and beautiful and the couple run towards each other in slow motion?

I almost giggled to myself when I had that thought, and that helped in a way, because when I came round the corner into the square I was still smiling. This smile – I hope – hid the shock I got just a moment later.

Ben was sitting, reading a paperback, on the low wall which runs round part of the square. He was wearing the jeans he wears to school but he had a new dark green shirt with the sleeves pushed up and showing his brown arms. He didn't look up as I approached and I had time to really stare at him, thinking to myself how fantastic he looked and how mad I was about him.

Suddenly though, horribly, *unbelievably,* I saw her: *Chelsea,* walking from the opposite corner of the square straight towards Ben. She looked across and saw me at exactly the same time as I saw her, and though a flicker of shock flashed across her face, her swingy, confident stride never faltered.

I don't know how I looked on the outside, whether *my* stride faltered, but I felt all the stuffing go out of my body and my legs go wobbly so that I could have just doubled up and collapsed in a heap. Only by a sheer effort did I keep the smile fixed on my face and keep walking towards Ben, one step in front of another automatically, like a robot.

He looked up just as we reached him.

'Hi!' he said, perfectly easily. And he looked from one to the other of us and smiled.

Chelsea tossed her hair – I could see she'd just washed it, because it was a bit frizzy – and sat down next to him. She was wearing a cropped white T-shirt and a tight skirt which was miles too short and showed off loads of leg. My first thought was that she looked tarty – and my second thought was that she looked slick and modern and that I, in my technicolour dream clothes, was stupidly over-dressed – an *Abba* lookalike.

Ben was sitting next to a concrete planter, and I wasn't going to sit down next to *her,* so I just stood there like a lemon. The silly smile was still on my face and I didn't know what to do with it. It didn't seem to be fading naturally but just stayed there, stuck.

They both looked up at me.

'So, what shall we do, then?' Ben asked. 'What is there to do around here on a Saturday?'

I just stared at him bleakly. I couldn't think of what to say, how to act, or what I was doing there at all. Why didn't someone tell me what was going on? I clung on to the crystal as if I was drowning, but I can't say it helped.

'We could go and have a hamburger, or we could walk by the river,' Chelsea said in a strangled voice.

I looked at her. She was talking like that beause she was trying not to laugh!

It was then that the smile disappeared altogether. I'd been set up! She was just having a laugh at my expense!

'How *could* you!' I gasped. 'You ... you ...' I wanted to call her all the awful names under the sun but the words wouldn't come. 'I hate you!' I burst out, and then I just turned on my heel, ran across the square and away from them both, my stupid long skirt getting tangled in my legs as I ran.

I hated her! I hated them both! I ran home, crying all the way. When I got in I went straight upstairs, locked myself in my room and tore down every single photograph that had Chelsea in it.

She'd got at him! She'd got at him with her flirty ways and she'd taken him away from me. She'd led him on and promised him – well, who knew what. Everything, probably.

She was a sly, treacherous *cow*. How could she do such a thing to me?

I *hated* her. Hated, despised and loathed her. She wasn't my best friend and she never would be again.

CHAPTER TWELVE

Saturday, 29th October

CHELSEA

'God, what was that all about?' Ben said as we watched Astra run across the square, clothes flying around her.

'I … I don't know,' I faltered.

'I mean – how did she get here? Did you tell her you were meeting me?'

'Of course not!' I said.

'She must have found out, then.' He shrugged his shoulders, 'somehow …'

I stared at the ground and swallowed hard. I felt *awful*. Someone must have told Astra about Ben and me – or perhaps Ben had told one of the boys and she'd overheard – and she'd decided to come and see for herself.

I nibbled at my lip worriedly, wondering what to do.

"I feel terrible,' I said to Ben. 'D'you think I ought to go after her?'

He raised his eyebrows. 'Why?'

'Because …' I swallowed, 'she thinks we did

it deliberately. She thinks I was laughing at her.'

'But you weren't.'

'No, I …well, it wasn't a real laugh. It was sort of hysterical – you know, when you don't know whether to laugh or cry.'

'Just leave her,' Ben said with a shrug. 'It's her problem, not ours."

'But …'

'She's a bit of a silly cow, isn't she?' he said bluntly. 'What did she expect? If she knew I was meeting you, she shouldn't have just turned up, should she?'

'What was it she said – something about us setting her up?

'Dunno,' he said. 'She was just raving on. She's jealous of you, that's all. That's what's behind it.'

'Is she?'

'Course. You've got the looks and you've got the style.'

'Have I?' I gulped. I'd thought she looked quite good, actually. Grunge and wild-child.

'I mean, what *was* she wearing? Outta date. Outta sight.'

I giggled nervously, disloyally.

He traced a line around my cheek with his finger. 'Whenever you get two friends together you get beauty … and you get the beast.'

'She's not *that* bad! She's quite pretty, really.'

'Not only that – you've got all the personality.'

'Oh, go on …'

'I just think she must have realised I was meeting you, and decided to turn up and spoil things,' he said.

'But why would she just appear? I can't believe anyone would just …'

'Perhaps you don't really know her,' Ben said. He put an arm round me. 'Look, can we forget about her? It's bad enough having her hang around at school all the time without having her on a date.'

'Yes. Sorry,' I said. 'It's just that she and I have gone round together for years and nothing like this has ever happened before. It's going to be really weird not being friends with her …'

Ben tipped up my face to his. 'Who's more important,' he asked, 'me or her?'

I didn't even have to think. 'You.'

'So forget about her.'

'OK,' I gulped.

He stood up. 'Let's go, then!'

We went. And though I tried to forget about Astra, it was difficult. I kept seeing her eyes as she looked from Ben to me and back again. I kept seeing her face crumple into tears.

I don't think this made me very good company. I did my best, though. We went to the shops and he bought a pair of jeans, and then I bought a skirt on Mum's storecard and bought him a jumper on it as well. Well, I knew Mum hardly ever bothered to check on what was on there. If she did, then I'd say it was for me.

I'd hoped that Ben and I would go on somewhere; have something to eat out, perhaps, or go to the Screen on the Hill, but when we came out of the shopping arcade he suddenly stopped dead.

I was asking him about where he lived at the time, trying to pin him down, quite sure that he must be in one of the Highate Road houses, when he suddenly looked at his watch.

'I've got to go now.'

I looked at him, bewildered. 'Why?'

'I've just remembered that I've got to be at home. Visitors – important visitors. I promised my dad.'

'I'll walk back with you, shall I?' I asked eagerly, wondering who they were, and if he'd ask me in.

He shook his head. 'No, you finish your shopping.'

'But when will I see you?' I said, forgetting to be cool. 'It's Sarah's party on Monday. D'you want to come round for me?'

'I'll ring you!' There was a shop doorway nearby and he suddenly pulled me into it and put both arms around me.

'I'll ring you tomorrow. OK?' he said into my ear.

I shivered all over. 'OK.'

'And until then ...' He gave me a brief smile and he kissed me, quite hard, quite swiftly, and then he just let me go and walked off, leaving me standing there.

I just stood there, stunned, feeling awkward and abandoned, not knowing what to do. I felt all mixed-up. I'd been kissed by a few boys before, but never like that. I'd never been kissed and just left standing.

Eventually, I caught the bus home. When I got in, Mum came out of the sitting room and asked me where I'd been.

'Shopping,' I said, not wanting to talk.

'Did you go with Astra?'

'No,' I said, wondering where this was leading. 'Why?'

'Because her mother's been on the phone. Apparently Astra went out shopping – her mother thought with you – but she came home early crying her eyes out.'

I didn't say anything.

'She won't talk about it and her mother thought you might know why.'

'It's nothing to do with me,' I said.

'Well, obviously not – if you haven't seen her.'

I opened my mouth and shut it again. I couldn't begin to tell Mum what had happened. She'd never understand. Not only that, she just wouldn't be interested.

'So who *have* you been with?'

I shrugged. 'A boy.'

'What boy?'

'Just a boy at school.' I started to walk up the stairs. 'Anyway, since when have you ever bothered about who I go round with?'

'As a matter of fact I take quite an interest in your friends,' she said. 'I don't like you hanging around the streets with just anyone.'

'Going shopping isn't hanging around the streets,' I said.

'And while we're on the subject of your friends, a boy came round for you last Sunday, while you were at Astra's. Name of Ben.'

I stopped at the top of the stairs. 'Why didn't you tell me?' And why hadn't *he* told me?

'Because I didn't like the look of him, that's why. I didn't want to encourage things.'

'What d'you mean? What are you talking about?'

'He's not the sort of boy I want you to be friends with. He's not from the same class as us,' she said.

'Oh, you snob!' I exploded. 'It might just interest you to know that his dad is an actor, they're stinking rich and they own the biggest house in the area!'

She sniffed. 'If you believe that, you'll believe anything.'

I went into my room and slammed the door.

'And that skirt's much too short,' she shouted after me.

I flung myself down on my bed. I didn't want her to spoil everything. I wanted to think about things: about Astra, about Ben, about the kiss.

After a moment I rolled on to my back and stared up at the ceiling, wondering what was going to happen between me and Astra? How would it be at school? Where were we going to sit in class? Should I make some sort of an effort to talk to her and straighten things out?

I got up and stared at the huge black and white poster over my desk which showed me and Astra with our arms around each other, killing ourselves laughing about something. It was our favourite photograph – Astra had had it blown up to poster size for my last year's Christmas present. It was mounted on white card and underneath Astra had captioned it: FRIENDS FOR EVER.

One by one, I took out the drawing pins which held it up. Then I rolled up the poster and put it under my bed. I didn't want any reminders of that friendship at the moment. I wasn't quite sure what was going to happen, but things had changed. My life was going to be different from now on, now that Ben was here. Maybe Astra would be in it. And maybe she wouldn't.

CHAPTER THIRTEEN

Sunday, 30th October

ASTRA

I couldn't be bothered to read the horoscopes in this morning's paper. I couldn't be bothered to do much, really. I just slopped about a bit and only came out of my room when Mum called up in a jolly voice to say that she hadn't seen me for *days* and was I still living there?

I went downstairs. She'd been cooking chocolate brownies and she gave me one warm from the oven.

'Chelsea loves these,' she said. 'She'll be round later for her weekly fix, I suppose.'

'No, she won't, actually,' I said.

Mum set down the baking tray and took off her oven gloves. 'So you two *have* had a row.'

'No, we haven't.'

'What's happened, then?'

I shook my head. I thought of Chelsea – and then I thought of Ben and I felt my eyes prickle with tears. I liked him so much and I'd really thought he liked me. I couldn't bear it if he didn't.

'What *is* it?' Mum sat herself down at the kitchen table. 'Come on, Astra. You and I usually talk our problems through, don't we?'

I nodded wordlessly.

'Well, then – tell me. That's what I'm here for. Nothing is so bad that you can't share it with your mum, you know.'

'I don't want to talk about it,' I muttered.

'Has Chelsea got another friend – is that it? Has she gone off with someone else?"

I nodded again. 'Gone off with someone else.'

'But *why?* I mean, did you have a row, or …'

'She's gone off with a boy,' I said flatly.

'Aah,' Mum said. 'I see.'

'No, you don't.' I took a deep breath. 'She and I both fancied the same boy – this new boy at school called Ben – but he liked me best and he asked me out but when I went to meet him yesterday she was there with him and she was laughing at me!'

'Oh, darling!' Mum said. She reached across the table to take my hand.

I pulled it away. 'Don't!' I didn't want her to feel sorry for me, I knew it would make me start crying again.

Mum shook her head. 'I can't think why she'd do such a thing to you. I mean, I know she's not exactly got a happy family life – her parents never seem to have much time for her – but I never thought she'd ever do the dirty on you.'

'There you go, then,' I said bitterly.

'But if this boy asked *you* out, why would she …'

'Mum!' I said. 'I don't want to talk about it, all right? I just don't want to talk about it!'

And I ran out of the kitchen and up to my room. I thought that yesterday had probably been the most miserable day I'd ever had in my life, but today didn't look like turning out much better.

I couldn't think what things were going to be like anymore. What would it be like at school without Chelsea? What would happen when we had to work on our projects together, when we weren't speaking? Suppose she got a new best friend? Suppose she told everyone about yesterday, about how I'd turned up and just burst into tears? Suppose she was with Ben every moment from now on, hanging round his neck? How was I going to cope?

And how was *he* going to act towards me now? Had he ever really liked me at all? I looked over to my Gemini parchment – what about us being compatible signs and the same astro-numbers and all that – didn't that count for anything?

I hugged my arms around myself and rocked on the bed, knowing that I'd never know what it felt like to be hugged by him. The worst thing was, though, *she* would …

The phone call came about four o'clock. I heard Mum answer it, and then she called up, 'Astra, call for you!'

My stomach turned over and over so that I felt sick. Ben or Chelsea? I didn't know who I wanted it to be. Either of them, really. Just as long as I had a chance with one. A boyfriend or a best friend …

Mum held her hand over the receiver. 'It's a boy,' she mouthed at me. 'Now, be sensible. Don't let …'

I took the phone off her. '*Please!* I said, making shooing movements with my hand. I turned my back on her and after a moment she went into the sitting room, closing the door quietly behind her.

'Hello?' I said uncertainly.

'Astra.' He said my name and I felt my knees go weak.

'Yes?'

'It's me. Ben.'

'I know.' I could see him there, see him standing with the phone to his ear, smiling slightly, green cat's eyes slanted.

'I've got something to tell you.'

'Yes?' I would try to be very cool and very controlled. I would listen to what he had to tell me without saying a word. I wouldn't let him see how hurt I was.

He didn't explain or apologise, though.

'I'm going away,' he said straight off.

'*What?*' Did he mean with Chelsea? Was that the secret they'd had? 'What d'you mean – going away?' I stammered.

'Look, I can explain everything. I need to talk to you.'

'Are you going away with Chelsea?' I asked fearfully.

He smiled, I could hear it in his voice. 'No,' he said.

A wave of relief washed across me. 'Who with, then? Who are you going with?'

'Depends,' he said.

'Will … will you be gone for long?'

'For ever, probably.'

'Oh.' I sat on the bottom of the stairs and closed my eyes. I didn't want to lose him, didn't want him to go. Even if he didn't want me, I still wanted him around. He *couldn't* just disappear from my life!

'I don't want you to go,' I said bleakly. I didn't care about yesterday, or about him and Chelsea. All I could think was that I wanted him to be there.

'I know you're hurt because of what happened yesterday.'

I was silent.

'I want to tell you why it happened. I want to take away the hurt.'

I still didn't say anything. There was a lump in my throat as big as a peach.

'If I was there now, Astra, I'd put my arms around you and explain everything. I'd kiss you and make you forget.'

I felt myself go hot all over. The receiver grew sweaty in my hand.

'I wish you weren't going,' I whispered. 'Do you *have* to?'

'You could always come with me,' he said.

'*What?*' I didn't think I'd heard right.

'You've always seemed a bit of a free spirit. How d'you fancy travelling?'

'What d'you mean – *run away?*'

'Yeah. Just come with me.'

'I couldn't!'

'So you don't care if you never see me again?'

'I do! I do, but …' I was horribly confused. 'What about yesterday. I thought you and Chelsea were …'

'As I said, I need to see you to explain. Chelsea was – well, you know what she's like –

a bit pushy.'

'Do you mean she just turned up?' I said. 'She found out you were meeting me and just …'

'Yeah – short skirt, tight T-shirt and all. Talk about being obvious. Look, if we talk, I'll explain everything. There's a lot you don't know. Things have been very difficult for me lately.' He gave a short laugh, 'I know it sounds crazy but you'll understand. My gran warned me that things were going to be difficult because of the position that Saturn's in at the moment.'

'Oh,' I said. 'So is that the reason you're going away?'

'That and the fact that my tarot has shown up lots of negative influences.'

I didn't know what to say.

'So d'you want to meet?' he asked.

'Now?' I asked.

'Not now. I can't get out right now.'

'Tomorrow? At Sarah's party?'

'I won't be at the party. I'll be gone by then.'

'But you can't just go!' I said, and added jealously, 'Are you sure Chelsea's not going with you?'

He laughed. 'I've just asked *you* to come with me, haven't I?'

'Yes, but …'

'And you've turned me down.'

'Do you mean you're going to ask both of us and see who takes you up on it?' I asked slowly.

He didn't answer that. 'Look, d'you want see me or not?'

'Of course I do,' I said in a small voice.

'I'll meet you in town tomorrow, then. You know that little park by the bus station? I'll see you there at eleven.'

'Will you be on your own?' I asked quickly. 'I mean, it will be just me there, won't it? I don't want what happened yesterday to ...'

'Got to go – money's running out,' he interrupted. 'And Astra – if you want to come with me, bring some money and your sleeping bag.'

The line went dead.

I stared at the receiver. He'd said he couldn't get out, but he was in a coin box. He'd said something about Saturn which was just a load of waffle. He'd said lots of things, but how did I know which were true and which weren't?

I went upstairs and lay down on my bed. I closed my eyes and saw the two of us, Ben and I, running away together. I saw us walking down a long, long dusty foreign road with our arms around each other. I saw us striding up a mountain in India, sitting on the edge of a lake. Free spirits.

Then I thought of Mum. I thought of home.

I opened my eyes. Of course I couldn't, *wouldn't* go with him – but if I didn't, then maybe Chelsea would. What if they ran away together and I never saw either of them again? How could I bear that?

What should I *do* …?

CHAPTER FOURTEEN

Sunday, 30th October

CHELSEA

I got up late and then watched a rerun of the Soaps I'd recorded, but didn't enjoy them as much as I usually did. About midday I heard mum come upstairs, so I turned off the TV and wandered into her bedroom.

She was packing bits and pieces into her sports bag. 'You'll be off to Astra's in a minute, won't you?' she said.

'No. I'm not going there today,' I said. 'Are you going to the gym? I could come with you if you like.'

She looked at me and frowned. 'Why aren't you going?'

I sighed. 'Because I'm not,' I said.

She raised an eyebrow.

'We've had a bit of a thing, if you must know. A bit of a falling out.'

'Oh?' She checked her hair. 'So what was that all about, then?'

'A boy,' I said.

'I didn't think Astra was interested in boys.'

'She wasn't.' But she is now, I thought.

'Oh well,' she shrugged. 'These things happen with people you think are your friends. I've always thought you were too much in each other's pockets, anyway. I daresay you'll find other friends easily enough.'

'I suppose so,' I said.

'Besides,' she went on, throwing her make-up bag into the sports holdall, 'you two would split up sooner or later anyway. You've only got another year at that school and then you can go somewhere more interesting.'

I knew what she meant by that. 'Somewhere where you'll meet a better sort of person,' she said. She picked up her holdall. 'See you later, then.'

'Hang on,' I said, 'I thought I'd come with you. I could have a swim or something.'

She looked at her watch. 'I've got a massage booked. You'd only be bored, waiting around. You can come with me one evening next week.'

And before I could say anything, she was down the stairs and into the car.

I was now seriously fed up. Dad was playing golf until late afternoon, so I went back into my own room and played a couple of CDs at top volume. Then I picked up the play I was supposed to be memorising, read a couple of pages of it and, bored to tears, shoved it to the bottom of my school bag.

I looked out of the window and sighed. Things used to be so easy. Why was everything going weird?

And why did I feel so hacked off, anyway? I was getting along great with Ben. He'd asked me out, he'd kissed me, he really seemed to fancy me – so *that* part of my life was all right.

No, it was the Astra bit that was wrong. But didn't everyone say that's what always happened – best friends were only best friends until a boy came along? That things always changed once a boy came on the scene?

The phone rang and I went into Mum and Dad's bedroom to answer it. It was Ben.

'Hi!' I said, really pleased to hear from him. 'D'you want to meet up?'

'Can't,' he said. 'There's big hassle going on here.'

'What?' I said. 'You mean at home – with your dad?'

There was a muffled noise, as if he had his hand over the mouthpiece and was speaking to someone else.

'Look,' he suddenly said bluntly, 'd'you fancy coming away with me?'

'What?' Had he really said that?!

'You and me. We could go to London. I've got some mates there; we could stay at their pads. I could get work in a club – I've got loads of contacts.'

'But ... well ... I don't know. What about everything here?'

'What's here? This is small town. It stinks! We want bright lights, don't we? You and I are made for something better than this.'

'Well, I ...' My heart began thudding with elation and fear. It was the wildest, craziest thing I'd ever heard of. But also the most exciting.

'Let's *do* something exciting!' Ben said, as if he was somehow picking up on what I was thinking. 'Come on. Let's go!'

'What about my mum and dad?' I said. 'They'll go mad.'

'Yeah, but if you're not here you won't know about it, will you? Anyway, I thought you said they didn't have much time for you."

'Yes, I know ...' I thought about it: about life with Ben, living in London, going to clubs, staying with his mates, living life to the full and not worrying about a thing. 'I know it sounds pretty good, but ...'

'It'd be fantastic! Us together. That's what you want, isn't it?'

'But we've hardly ... I mean, shouldn't we at

least meet and talk about it first?'

'There's no time for that. Seize the moment – isn't that what they say? Look, I'm going away tomorrow morning. Definite. Either you come with me or you don't.'

'I can't decide that quickly!' I said in a panic.

'Take it or leave it, Chelsea. Look, meet me tomorrow in that park near the bus garage at eleven. You can come with me – or you can kiss me goodbye.'

The line went dead.

I went back into my room and looked around. All my stuff! How could I leave my clothes and my CDs and all my possessions? How could I leave at all?

Life with Ben. I shivered excitedly. What would it be like? I had visions of smokey clubs, pop stars, restaurants and glam places …

Mum came back from her massage, then Dad came in from golf and we had something to eat, and all the time I was thinking that maybe this could be the last time I'd sit here with them, eating a meal and hardly speaking. Soon I could be leading another, different, wild and exciting life …

A bit after that, up in my room, I started to think about Astra, about how *she'd* feel if Ben and I ran off together. For years she'd been my truly best friend, the least I could do would be to tell her I was going. If I was.

It was quite late when I rang her and I think her mum was a bit surprised it was me. 'I missed you today, Chelsea,' she said. 'I cooked chocolate brownies, too!'

'Oh well, save me one,' I said awkwardly.

'See you tomorrow, will we?'

''Spect so,' I mumbled.

Astra was ages coming to the phone, and she said hello so quietly that I could hardly hear it.

'I rang to … I thought I'd better tell you that Ben's rung me,' I said. 'He's going away. He's asked me to go with him and well, I don't know that I will but …'

She gave a little cry. 'He's asked me to go away with him, too!'

'What?' I was bewildered. 'Why?'

'What d'you mean – why? Why has he asked you, come to that?'

'But he said … I don't understand …'

There was a long silence. 'Nor do I,' she said. 'There's things going on here we don't know about.'

'I know all about him!' I said quickly.

'*Do* you?' she said. 'Well, you haven't exactly been honest with me, have you?'

'You can talk!'

'OK, I suppose we're both a bit guilty of

that.' There was another long silence. 'Are you going?"

'Yes,' I said.

'Going away with him?!' she said incredulously. 'Running away?!'

'I didn't mean that. I meant I'm going to meet him tomorrow.'

'Eleven o'clock?' she said. 'In the park by the bus garage?'

'That's it. Are you going as well?'

'I think so.'

'But not going away with him?'

She gave a bitter little laugh. 'Well, we can't *both* go, can we?'

I didn't say anything else, and neither did she. After about a minute I just put the phone down.

And then I went to bed and didn't sleep at all.

CHAPTER FIFTEEN

Monday, 31st October, 11.00 a.m.

ASTRA, CHELSEA AND BEN

It's just on eleven o'clock and, although it's half-term, there's no one else on the green by the bus garage except Astra and Chelsea.

Astra is wearing a long skirt and her old jacket. She carries a bulky plastic carrier bag which might, or might not, contain overnight things.

Chelsea has her hair up, is wearing full make-up and, despite it being quite cold, wears a cropped top and miniskirt. At her feet is one of her mum's leather sports bags which may, perhaps, contain a few items of clothing. Then again, Chelsea might have the bag with her because she's going to her mum's gym later.

'Perhaps he won't come,' Chelsea says. It's the first thing either girl has said to the other.

Astra makes a little noise midway between a giggle and a sigh. 'Maybe he won't. Maybe he's gone already.'

'With someone else!' Chelsea says wildly.

They both laugh and then feel awkward and look away. It's ages since they shared a joke.

Another minute goes by. Astra nods towards Chelsea's sports bag and says, 'Are you … you know? Would you really?'

Chelsea taps the bag with her foot. 'Hmm …' she says, which doesn't exactly tell anyone anything. She looks at Astra piercingly. 'Would you? *Are* you?'

Astra takes a deep breath, but is saved from replying because Ben is walking across the park towards them. He's wearing an old denim jacket and has a rucksack over one shoulder. He walks easily, half-smiling to himself, looking just as he looked when he'd walked into their lives: cool.

'Hi, girls,' he says. 'I guessed you'd get it together."

'Where are you going?' Chelsea blurts out.

'Why *now?*' says Astra, who looks as if she might burst into tears at any minute.

'I told you,' Ben says to her, 'destiny and all that.' He points upwards, 'the planets move in mysterious ways."

Chelsea screws up her face. 'What are you talking about?'

'His granny,' Astra murmurs. 'She's psychic.'

Chelsea continues to look bewildered. 'I

thought you were going away because of your dad – because of the boarding school business.'

It's Astra's turn to look confused.

Ben says nothing, so Chelsea explains. 'Ben's dad wants him to go to this flash boarding school,' she says.

'I didn't know you lived with your dad!' Astra exclaims.

'His dad's a famous actor,' Chelsea says in a *didn't you even know that* voice.

'What?'

Ben swings his rucksack off his shoulder and puts it down.

'So what's the truth about me? Who knows? More to the point, who's coming with me? Either of you?' He laughs, '*Both* of you?'

For a while neither girl speaks. Each is looking at the other and thinking: Would I really go? Would *she* go? What's going to *happen*?

Chelsea says, 'Before either of us says we're going, we ought to know who we're going with. So what's the truth about you? Who are you, exactly?'

Ben laughs. 'My name is …' he hesitates, 'No. I don't think I'll tell you my name.'

'You mean it's not Ben Adams?' Chelsea asks incredulously, while Astra thinks about the name-number match which now doesn't match at all.

'And I suppose you're not a Gemini, either!' Astra says.

'Haven't got the faintest idea,' says Ben easily. 'Never taken the slightest bit of interest in all that stuff.'

'But you said … your gran and everything.'

Ben doesn't reply, just smiles.

There is another silence, then Chelsea says, 'Is your dad really an actor?'

'Dunno,' Ben shrugs. 'He might be. I've never had a dad – not to speak of.'

'But where d'you come from, then?' Astra asks.

Ben looks from one girl to the other. 'Nowhere. Anywhere. I've been sleeping rough all summer, and then they caught up with me and stuck me into this foster home place. And I got fed up with that so now I'm off again. They can't keep me. Free as a bird, me!'

'Is that why you didn't want to bump into any social workers at school?' Astra asks.

'Is that why you didn't really go and see the school secretary?' Chelsea says. 'But why come to school at all, then?'

Ben shrugs. 'Didn't have much choice,' he says. 'At this Home they sometimes used to drive me to school – and anyway, I had to go *somewhere* during the day, didn't I? I figured that as long as I didn't actually enrol there, though, no one would be able to keep tabs on me.'

'But why did you say all those things to us?' Astra bursts out. 'Why did you make up all those stories about yourself?'

Ben shrugs. 'Why not? It was something to do.'

'You just … just amused yourself with us?' Chelsea says.

'Something like that. It helped to pass the time. Anyone can be anything he wants to be, remember?'

Astra starts crying quietly.

'OK,' Ben says, spreading his hands. 'I was bored, right. I walk into a school and I get two girls making sheeps eyes at me: two best friends, both a bit gullible. And then I think, look at these two: they're set up. They've got homes and they've got families and they've got friends – all the things that I've never had. And I think maybe it would be a laugh to split up these two friends, just to see if I can …'

'You did it *deliberately*?!' Astra asks. 'You did it for a laugh? You saw us and you set out to break up our friendship?'

'Didn't you fancy either of us?' Chelsea cries.

'Either. Both.' Ben shrugs. 'Girls are ten a

penny. I thought I'd see if I could land you – and you weren't exactly difficult to hook. Either of you.'

'But I wasn't going to run away with you!' Astra says hotly.

'Nor was I!' says Chelsea.

Ben looks at them, and then he looks at their bags and laughs. 'No?' He picks up his rucksack. 'See you around, then.'

He walks off and then he calls over his shoulder. 'Nice to know you. And next time, don't believe everything you're told, right?"

Astra and Chelsea stare after him. He reaches the pavement at the edge of the green but he doesn't turn to wave.

Chelsea sinks down to sit on the sports bag. Astra just stands there, head hanging, arms folded round herself.

'You sent him a card,' Astra says. 'What was that all about?'

Chelsea looks at her sharply. 'How did you know that?'

'I ... well, I saw it.'

'I lent him some money,' Chelsea says, and then she gives a harsh laugh. 'Well, I suppose I should say I *gave* him some money.' She sighs, 'I was easy pickings.'

'But I thought, I really thought ...' Astra murmurs.

'So did I!' says Chelsea. She looks up at Astra. 'We've both been really stupid, haven't we?'

'Gullible …' Astra says slowly.

'We believed everything he told us.'

'We put him before *us*,' Astra says. 'Before our friendship.'

'I know. We shouldn't have done that.'

Astra blows her nose, then she says, 'Is it too late, d'you think?'

'Too late to be best friends again?'

Astra nods.

'I suppose we could try,' says Chelsea.

'Wonder where he'll go?' Astra says wistfully.

'Wonder where he's been!' Chelsea says, and she stands up and picks up the sports bag.

The two girls begin to walk across the green together, through the chip wrappings and drinks cans. Neither of them are quite sure enough of the other to suggest that they go for a walk, spend some time together, talk things over, but it's in both their minds to do so.

Maybe by the time they reach the edge of the park they'll speak about it, and then maybe they'll go off together and things will be back to normal.

At least on the surface …